Moving Targets

Slocum fell into the easy rhythm of the horse, warmed by Suzanne's arms around him and her body pressing tightly against his. The shot that sang through the still, early morning took him completely by surprise.

"Hang on," he called to Suzanne. She lurched and almost tumbled from horseback as he bent forward and put his spurs to his horse's flanks. Barely had the horse run a dozen yards when another shot rang out.

Slocum went sailing through the air, Suzanne still clinging to him. His horse's front legs crumpled and its head hit the ground. After that, Slocum wasn't sure what happened. He skidded along the road on his belly with Suzanne clinging to him. By the time he came to a halt, Slocum was torn up and bloody and madder than hell.

He stood and the dark-haired woman slid to one side, sitting in the dirt and staring numbly at him.

"Stay down," he snarled. Slocum slapped leather. His Colt Navy came easily to his hand, but he could not find a target . . .

DON'T MISS THESE
ALL-ACTION WESTERN SERIES
FROM THE BERKLEY PUBLISHING GROUP

THE GUNSMITH by J. R. Roberts
Clint Adams was a legend among lawmen, outlaws, and ladies. They called him . . . the Gunsmith.

LONGARM by Tabor Evans
The popular long-running series about Deputy U.S. Marshal Custis Long—his life, his loves, his fight for justice.

SLOCUM by Jake Logan
Today's longest-running action Western. John Slocum rides a deadly trail of hot blood and cold steel.

BUSHWHACKERS by B. J. Lanagan
An action-packed series by the creators of Longarm! The rousing adventures of the most brutal gang of cutthroats ever assembled—Quantrill's Raiders.

DIAMONDBACK by Guy Brewer
Dex Yancey is Diamondback, a Southern gentleman turned con man when his brother cheats him out of the family fortune. Ladies love him. Gamblers hate him. But nobody pulls one over on Dex . . .

WILDGUN by Jack Hanson
The blazing adventures of mountain man Will Barlow—from the creators of Longarm!

TEXAS TRACKER by Tom Calhoun
J. T. Law: the most relentless—and dangerous—manhunter in all Texas. Where sheriffs and posses fail, he's the best man to bring in the most vicious outlaws—for a price.

JAKE LOGAN

SLOCUM'S BAR-S RANCH

JOVE BOOKS, NEW YORK

THE BERKLEY PUBLISHING GROUP
Published by the Penguin Group
Penguin Group (USA) Inc.
375 Hudson Street, New York, New York 10014, USA
Penguin Group (Canada), 90 Eglinton Avenue East, Suite 700, Toronto, Ontario M4P 2Y3, Canada
(a division of Pearson Penguin Canada Inc.)
Penguin Books Ltd., 80 Strand, London WC2R 0RL, England
Penguin Group Ireland, 25 St. Stephen's Green, Dublin 2, Ireland (a division of Penguin Books Ltd.)
Penguin Group (Australia), 250 Camberwell Road, Camberwell, Victoria 3124, Australia
(a division of Pearson Australia Group Pty. Ltd.)
Penguin Books India Pvt. Ltd., 11 Community Centre, Panchsheel Park, New Delhi—110 017, India
Penguin Group (NZ), 67 Apollo Drive, Rosedale, North Shore 0632, New Zealand
(a division of Pearson New Zealand Ltd.)
Penguin Books (South Africa) (Pty.) Ltd., 24 Sturdee Avenue, Rosebank, Johannesburg 2196,
South Africa

Penguin Books Ltd., Registered Offices: 80 Strand, London WC2R 0RL, England

This is a work of fiction. Names, characters, places, and incidents either are the product of the author's imagination or are used fictitiously, and any resemblance to actual persons, living or dead, business establishments, events, or locales is entirely coincidental.

SLOCUM'S BAR-S RANCH

A Jove Book / published by arrangement with the author

PRINTING HISTORY
Jove edition / January 2009

ISBN: 978-0-515-14571-7

JOVE®
Jove Books are published by The Berkley Publishing Group,
a division of Penguin Group (USA) Inc.
375 Hudson Street, New York, New York 10014.
JOVE® is a registered trademark of Penguin Group (USA) Inc.
The "J" design is a trademark of Penguin Group (USA) Inc.

PRINTED IN THE UNITED STATES OF AMERICA

10 9 8 7 6 5 4 3 2 1

1

John Slocum rode into Middle Park on the western slope of the Rocky Mountains, thinking it was a lovely day. And it was. A lovely day filled with bullets, all directed at him.

The first shot tore a piece out of his canvas duster. The second sent his black, floppy-brimmed hat snapping back on his head, caught and held only by the string he had fastened under his chin. The sudden bite of that string reminded him too much of a hangman's noose. Another bullet, which spooked his horse and caused the roan to rear, removed such thoughts of dangling by the neck, and replaced them with the need just to keep from getting filled with lead.

He fought his horse and got it under control, only to have a rifleman on the opposite side of the road open up on him. The horse reared and threw him. Slocum landed hard on his back and spent a few seconds staring open-eyed at the bright blue Colorado sky stretching in an unbroken dome above him. Then dust began billowing all around as more slugs sought a permanent home in his body.

The fall dazed him, and he had a difficult time figuring which way to dodge. Men with six-shooters on his left side and at least one sniper with a rifle on his right made the decision one of life and death. All he saw of his horse was a slowly settling dust cloud down the road. The pounding he heard might have been the roan's hooves or it could have been the blood rushing in his ears. Reacting more out of instinct than logic, Slocum got to his feet and fell forward into a ditch alongside the road. During rainy season, it probably ran full. Since it was late summer, all that remained was dust, more dust, and weeds that poked at his face until he sneezed. He tried to hold back another pollen-caused sneeze, but his situation got worse by the instant.

The men—there had to be at least four—on his left were moving closer, firing steadily as they came. They worked together better than a posse. They might have been a military unit on foot, some shooting while the rest reloaded. That way, they maintained a curtain of lead in front of them and kept anyone stupid enough to be there flat on his face. Worse, the way they moved, two were always covering their partners. This tactic stole away any chance Slocum had to drop even one of them and improve his odds.

If he tried getting to the other side of the road, the rifleman would take him out. Try as he might, he could not find where the sniper hid even to throw a couple slugs his way.

Slocum rolled onto his side, drew his Colt Navy, and waited to take his first shot. He cocked the six-gun, but did not fire when he saw a hat poke above a rock twenty feet away. They wanted him to waste his ammo shooting at a hat intentionally raised on a stick. Slocum arched his back and looked in a different direction in time to see two men trying to get him in a box. He was already caught in a cross fire. They wanted to get south of him, cut off escape, and fire from all directions.

His first shot hit a man in the leg and sent him to the ground, grunting in pain. His next two bullets fell right for a kill on the outlaw accompanying the wounded man. He didn't see what happened to that owlhoot, but there was neither sound nor return gunfire.

"He got Ned! The damn varmint's done kilt Ned!"

Slocum paid no heed to the words. They were intended to make him careless. Some men might have felt elation at the idea he had shot one of his attackers. Slocum would savor that feeling only when they were all ready for a simple grave in a potter's field.

Two more quick shots added extra lead to the man he had hit in the leg earlier. He couldn't be certain, but thought he had about blown off the man's leg. Even if the son of a bitch didn't bleed to death, he wouldn't be a factor in the fight.

Slocum took advantage of the lull in the fight to fumble out a few cartridges from his pocket as the other men he faced hesitated. They had thought to roll over him and probably rob him. If he had been able to discuss the matter, he would have easily convinced them he was so broke he didn't have two nickels to rub together. Worse, he had left Gunnison owing a powerful lot of money to a crooked gambler. Slocum wasn't sure he had been cheated, but it didn't much matter. Moving on was easier than listening to the tinhorn gambler gloat about how he had drawn to an inside straight and won.

Reloaded six-gun in hand, Slocum considered his options. He could go south along the road he had cleared with his accurate gunfire and hope to find his horse eventually. There was only one problem with this sensible scheme. To do that exposed his back. If he crossed the road, the hidden sniper would take him out.

That limited his options to one. He attacked. Slocum got his feet under him and dug the toes of his boots into the rocky ground the best he could to launch himself forward. He headed for the boulder where the hat had been thrust up. He swarmed over and found nothing but footprints in the soft earth.

Slocum kept running, following that distinctive trail. He burst out of the tumble of rocks to where a pair of men argued. Neither saw him coming. He had taken them by surprise. His six-shooter blared out four rounds, two for each man. One shot each would have been enough.

Still moving, Slocum skirted the small clearing and hunted for others. The best he could tell, there had only been four trying to ventilate him from this side of the road. However, he counted tracks from six horses. Two more of the owlhoots were out there.

One had to be the rifleman. Maybe the other had back-tracked to be sure Slocum didn't have a partner riding to catch up. His guesses fell apart when he heard at least two six-guns firing with what had to be return fire from the rifle.

Slocum reloaded and made his way back to the men he had cut down. A quick search yielded twenty dollars in scrip and no clue who they might be. He tucked the money into his shirt pocket, then picked up their pistols. If he had to get himself in a protracted gunfight, by damn but he wasn't going to waste his own ammo.

A six-gun in each hand, he got back to the road and tried to locate the sniper up in the rocks. He caught the briefest flash of a man on a horse heading into the hills, swinging a six-shooter around as he rode like all the demons of Hell nipped at his heels. Slocum couldn't be certain what he actually saw, though. The only thing he knew for sure was that if it was human and moved, he would try to gun it down before it got him.

This wasn't the kind of fight where he had to worry about friends.

Sucking in his breath and letting it out slowly calmed him a little. Then he ran as hard as he could across the road and found another ditch to dive into. This one lacked the hip-high weeds, but sported brutal thistles that tore at his face and hands. Ignoring the nettles, he looked for a spot to make a stand. A lone cottonwood tree fifty feet away had to be enough.

Slocum ran. Bullets tore at him as he dodged. One grazed his cheek and left a bloody, inconsequential gash. By the time he reached the safety of the thirty-foot-tall cottonwood, he was mad all over again. He settled down and tried to make sense out of everything around him.

The occasional slug that knocked splinters off the tree trunk made him wary, and caused him to take longer getting the lay of the land than was his wont. When he did, he gripped the two six-shooters he had taken from the outlaws and ran straight for an arroyo at the base of a hill. He got there without anyone taking a potshot at him.

He listened hard and knew the tide of battle was changing fast. The rifle fire came sporadically now, as if the sniper was hoarding his ammunition. The flatter crack of handguns did not let up. The two men going after the sniper must have a pack mule weighed down with cartridges to be so profligate.

Moving carefully, Slocum made his way up the hill and found himself looking down into a draw. When a horseman slowly rode past, Slocum stepped out and blazed away with both captured six-guns. The rider toppled to the ground without making a sound.

"You figgered it out yet, Glasgow?" The question came from higher on the hillside, about where Slocum reckoned the sniper to be holed up. "I got reinforcements. You and me and my boys. Don't like them odds, do you?"

Slocum reacted when a second rider galloped past. His six-shooters came up empty fast, and he went for his ebony-handled Colt Navy. Barely had he cleared leather when the rifleman took the rider out of the saddle. Slocum saw a tiny fountain of blood at the back of the rider's head before he crumpled forward. The runaway horse quickly took its dead rider out of sight.

"You willin' to call a truce, mister?" the sniper shouted.

"I never wanted to be in this fight," Slocum called back. He knew better than to step out into the line of fire. He thought he understood all that had happened, but he could be wrong. Those weren't deputies or lawmen of any kind. He pegged them as road agents. That didn't mean the man on the hillside was pure as the wind-driven snow. The outlaws might have had a falling-out.

"I cain't come down to you, so you got to come to me."

"Tell you what," Slocum called. "I've got a better idea. I'll leave. You go your way, and I'll go mine." He looked over his shoulder at the road leading southward. His roan must have run itself out by now. It might be several miles away, but he could retrieve it before sundown if he got lucky.

"Then you're signin' my death warrant. Them rustlers drilled me through both legs. No way I can even drag myself along."

"Throw out your rifle."

"Why should I trust you?"

"See you in Hell," Slocum said. He had no hankering to argue the matter.

"Wait, mister, confound you, wait a goddamn minute!" The rifle clattered against a rock and slid a few feet. "My six-shooter is empty." A pistol followed. "I got a knife, too, but it's got a buckhorn handle and tossing it into the rocks'll chip its damned hilt."

Slocum was already moving, heading back around the hill and making his way upward in a spiral path to come out behind the man. By the time the man was cursing a blue streak, Slocum spotted him. He was hunched over, his shoulders and back making him appear to be a human question mark. His hands were trembling and wizened, and the only part of the man Slocum could tell that was in good shape was his mouth. Not once did he repeat a curse.

"I suppose I could let you go on. I'm getting quite an education in cussing," Slocum said. The old man twisted about. Slocum saw that he had not lied about his injuries. Blood soaked both pants legs.

"I done what I said. If you're one of them sons of bitches, go on and kill me." The man made an obscene gesture.

"I got caught in the cross fire. Who were they? Outlaws?"

"Rustlers, each and ever' last one. Coldhearted killers.

Not content with stealin' a man's cows. They want to kill the one what owns the cows, too."

"You were out hunting the rustlers?"

"Hell, no, I was out tryin' to figger why my lazy cowboys wasn't able to round up 'nuff cows for us to even have steak for dinner. I ran into them varmints. Goddamn them all."

"Probably," Slocum said. "They're all certainly on their way to Hell."

"You kilt the lot of them?"

"They shouldn't have fired on me." Slocum knew at least one had ridden off, but he wasn't inclined to worry over details at the moment.

"I shot at you, thinkin' you was one of 'em," the man said. His leathery face contorted into what Slocum guessed was a smile. "My name's Jackson Wimmer, and I own the biggest damn spread in all of Middle Park."

"The biggest?" Slocum looked skeptical, and the old man grinned even more.

"Maybe not the *biggest* but certainly the best."

Slocum had to laugh. "That I'll buy." When he saw Wimmer wince as he tried to move, he knew the old man was in bad shape. "I'll rustle up a couple horses and get you to a doctor."

"Rustle? Hell, no, steal 'em if you have to, but don't go sayin' that word round me. Makes me mad. All the time I hear 'rustlers' and it always means I lost me another hunnerd head of beeves. Horse thievin's just fine, but no rustlin'."

Slocum took the better part of an hour catching two of the outlaws' horses and leading them back up the hill to where Wimmer lay. At first, Slocum thought the old rancher had upped and died, but he proved to be of sterner stuff.

"Cain't climb into the saddle. Might be you could toss me across a saddle like a bag o' flour?"

"That'd kill a healthy man, riding like that," Slocum said. "Better if I tied you upright."

"You're a big, strappin' fella. Reckon you can hoist me into the saddle if I give you some help?"

Slocum lifted the old man more easily than he had thought. Wimmer was nothing but a bag of bones. He wobbled in the saddle but held on gamely. After he was astride the horse, Slocum did what he could for the old man's shot-up legs. From the look of it, a single bullet had entered the left thigh and come out on the right side. Other than this wound, Wimmer was in decent enough shape.

"Which way do we ride?" Slocum mounted and looked at the road with some longing. He had nothing drawing him southward, but his roan was in that direction along with his gear.

"Back north, from the direction you were ridin'," Wimmer said. Slocum looked at him sharply. There was a drop of acid in the old man's tone, as if he took some delight in putting Slocum out.

"Is there a town nearby with a doctor? You need those holes in your legs tended."

"You did a fine job bandagin' me up. You wouldn't happen to be a doctor now, would you, Slocum?"

"I do what I can but never thought of myself that way." Slocum turned away, memories flooding back on him about the time he had been forced to act as a doctor during the war. His friends had been killed left and right. The Federals had overrun an artillery position and turned the cannon against the Rebs. Slocum's entire unit had been wiped out, leaving only him. A field doctor had ordered him to help with the wounded—and not just to carry off the dead and stack them like cordwood. Slocum had assisted the doctor in hacking off arms and legs in a filthy surgery tent. He reckoned they killed more between them, the doctor and him, than the Federals had using the cannon at point-blank range.

There had always been a dozen more wounded waiting for them that day, no matter how long they worked. Slocum was no stranger to bullet wounds, but he could never think of himself as a doctor after that endless day. He had felt more like a butcher.

"You got the look of a man able to do a lot of things purty good."

Slocum shrugged.

"You wear that hogleg of yours slung in a cross-draw holster like you know how to use it. You a gunfighter?"

"Just a drifter."

"You kin use that gun of yours and you don't shy from a fight," Wimmer said. The old man fixed him with a gimlet eye. The body might be frail, but the mind was sharp and appraising. "You kin ride and rope, too, betcha."

"Done my fair share." Slocum found himself telling Jackson Wimmer about the numerous cattle drives he had been on from Texas up to the railheads in Kansas.

"You ever boss one of them drives?"

"Trail boss on one, ramrod on another," Slocum said. "About the only thing I never did was be a cook. The way I'd've fixed chuck would have given everybody bellyaches. No work would have gotten done. Might have even gotten lynched."

Wimmer laughed at this. "A wise man knows his limitations."

"You including yourself in that or excluding?" Slocum asked.

"Nobody's ever called me a wise man. Worse. Always worse."

"You a mean drunk?" Slocum asked.

"What's that supposed to mean?"

Slocum reached back in the saddlebags and rummaged about until he found the half-pint of whiskey that had sloshed so loud it had drawn his attention for nigh on a mile. He pulled the cork and took a swig. It burned at his mouth and throat but went down good. Passing it over to Wimmer, he watched the man's eyes fix on the bottle.

"Ain't 'nuff there to git me drunk," Wimmer complained.

He drained the rest of the bottle and tossed it away. The glass shattered loudly when it hit a large rock alongside the road.

Slocum hoped the liquor would ease some of the pain etched on the man's face. Wimmer said nothing, but he was weakening fast. A man half his age would have been in trouble, yet the rancher refused to slow down or take more than a few minutes' rest.

"You got family to look after you?" Slocum asked.

"Ain't got family. Hardly have any ranch hands no more either," Wimmer said. "Cowards. The lot of 'em are cowards. They all run off when the rustlers moved in on us."

"What's the law doing about them?"

"Cain't do much. From what I kin tell, them rustlers are 'bout half white and half Ute."

"You mean breeds?"

"No, you idiot. I mean some of 'em are white men and some are redskins."

"That there's the road to your ranch," Slocum said. A neatly carved sign with Wimmer's name in white-painted lettering showed the way off the road and back into a wide valley. "Don't fall off before you get there."

"Hold on. Where the hell're you goin', Slocum?"

"Somewhere that crotchety old men don't call me an idiot."

"You prefer me callin' you a son of a bitch?" Wimmer eyed him carefully.

"Yeah."

"I promise not to call you an idiot again."

"That promise doesn't mean a whole lot since I'm riding back to find my roan as soon as I see you to your house."

"Find your damned horse, but you got a whole lot more of me to put up with."

"How's that?" Slocum saw the expression on Jackson Wimmer's face and could not figure out what it was. Something sly, but also something else, as if he was on the point of begging.

"It wouldn't be right for my foreman to ride off and never come back."

Slocum hadn't known what Wimmer was going to say, but this took him completely by surprise.

2

"So you git them beeves moved into a better pasture?" Jackson Wimmer glared at Slocum.

"Did that yesterday. Have the boys putting up a new corral right now. Your old one was falling down. It's a wonder you didn't lose more horses just from taking it into their heads to walk off."

"You might call me sir when you address me."

"I'm your foreman, not your slave," Slocum said. He stared at Wimmer and wondered how an old man with such a tongue ever put together a spread like this. It had amused Slocum, for a day or so, that the ranch carried the Bar-S name. About where that brand had come from, Wimmer was silent although Slocum had asked. Somewhere in the back of his mind, he made a small joke that it was named after him. The Bar-S for the Bar-Slocum Ranch. It had taken less than a week for this notion to fade away and no longer amuse him, mostly because there was no one to share the joke with. The cowboys working for him were as surly as their employer, and nowhere near as competent, except a couple who might prove decent cowboys someday, if they ever got off their cracker asses and worked longer than a few minutes at a time. Slocum had looked over the books and seen that the Bar-S made money most years. Even in as lush a place as Middle Park with pastureland everywhere, making a profit was always a problem.

The rustlers added to the losses. The prior year Wimmer had lost a considerable portion of his herd to some disease that Slocum reckoned to be splenic fever. Even then, the Bar-S had broken even. Weather and disease were things Wimmer took in stride as being forces of nature, but the rustlers were another matter.

"For what I'm payin' you, I deserve respect," Wimmer groused.

"For what you're paying me, I ought to get on my horse and ride till its legs fall off, hoping never to see you again," Slocum said.

"A week on the job and already you're gettin' uppity."

Jackson Wimmer winced as he tried to shift position on the sofa in the parlor. He was pale under his weather-beaten hide, but there was no trace of fever from his gunshots. He looked to be wasting away, but that didn't come from shooting it out with the outlaws.

"You need a housekeeper to boss around," Slocum said. "Maybe then you'd let me be so I could do my job."

"I need to know what's goin' on out there," Wimmer said.

"You want to meddle. I can run this spread." Slocum saw from Wimmer's reaction that was what the old man feared most. He wanted to be indispensable. Knowing that a younger man was as capable, if not more so, rankled worse than being laid up with bullet wounds. Those shot-up legs probably wore down on Wimmer, too, with a constant reminder. The very rustlers he tried to stop had laid him up. Worse, he'd only accounted for one of them. Slocum had cut the rest of them down to size.

"You call it meddlin', I call it lookin' after my business."

"You should have done better hiring ranch hands," Slocum said. "They're a pitiful lot."

"Had better," Wimmer said sullenly. "Most of the good ones upped and left, like you're threatenin' to do."

"Fancy that. Why'd any self-respecting man take your shit and not get paid better for it?" Slocum heard a fight outside in the yard and itched to go settle it. The cowboys working the Bar-S were worse than he let on to Wimmer, but the man had to know the caliber of those who worked for him. The top hand, Colorado Pete Kelso, spent as much time drunk as he did sober, if the sober times were counted as when he passed out. For two days Slocum had tried to figure out what particular skills Colorado Pete had that qualified him to do anything more than muck the stables. Unless Slocum looked a lot harder, he wasn't likely to find the man's real talents.

"Why'd you take the job, if you think I'm such a skin-flint?"

"I needed the aggravation," Slocum said. "Wasn't enough out there." He saw the small smile come to Wimmer's lips. It vanished almost instantly, replaced by a look of pure pain. "Let me get on into town and fetch the doctor. You need more looking after than I can deliver."

"No!" The word came explosively. Wimmer's watery eyes sharpened with anger and he half sat up, in spite of his obvious pain. "You do somethin' dumb like that and you can get on your horse and ride. Won't pay you, will charge you for your room and board whilst you been here."

"Don't like the doctor much?"

"Don't go pryin' where there's no cause, Slocum. You got work to do, don't you? Why ain't you out there doin' it then? Them boys'll like on to kill one another if you don't do somethin' about the fightin'."

"Because a cranky old man wanted to waste my time," Slocum said.

He left, and saw that the fight between two men had drawn quite a crowd. The Bar-S had twelve hands. Six of them, including Colorado Pete, circled the two fighting. They swung hard and if either had landed one of those blows, the other would have ended up dead. Both men were drunk, and the fight was more of a grunting match. They grappled and shoved and mostly tried to keep from falling down.

"Don't, Slocum. Let 'em fight it out. There's been bad blood 'twixt 'em for a month," said Colorado Pete.

Slocum hesitated. The top hand might be right. Sometimes a fight settled the dust and drained off animosity that otherwise festered into gunplay. He hadn't been on the Bar-S long enough to know.

"How much have those two had to drink?" Slocum peered up at the sky. The sun was barely past noon.

"What's it to you?"

Slocum turned from the men tentatively fighting and squared off with Colorado Pete.

"I'm foreman and I asked you a question. If you're top hand, you have two choices. Answer or get the hell off the Bar-S."

"No need to get testy," Colorado Pete said, looking away. The way his hand twitched near his six-gun made Slocum wary. He doubted Kelso would throw down on him, but from what he had seen, it was more likely the cowboy might consider shooting him in the back.

"No more booze until after evening chuck from now on," Slocum said. "The next man who's drunk before then gets kicked out of the company."

"You'll lose the lot of 'em," Colorado Pete warned.

"Then I'll have enough money to hire a couple cowboys able to do all their jobs." Slocum was past caring what Colorado Pete or any of the others thought of him. In a way, he admired Jackson Wimmer, but the old man's hiring practices left a lot to be desired.

"Whatever you say, Slocum."

"Break it up!" Slocum bellowed, and got the attention of the men in the circle as well as those fighting. "You two got a lot of piss and vinegar in you. Time to turn it against the rustlers. Both of you, saddle up. Bring along rifles. We're going hunting for rustlers."

The men pushed away from each other, wary of a sneak attack, then looked at Slocum with complete disbelief.

"You cain't mean it. We ain't deputies to go trackin' down rustlers."

"I can track. You two will do the shooting, if it comes to that. Mount up."

Slocum brushed past Colorado Pete and went to the barn. The roan stood nervously in a stall as he entered. Slocum gave it a carrot, calmed it, and then saddled. Although he took better than ten minutes, he still ended up waiting for the other two.

They eventually rode up, apprehensive.

"You makin' us kill rustlers, Slocum?"

Slocum tried to remember the man's name. He had been introduced to the whole sorry lot, but had forgotten their names as soon as he heard them.

"If it comes down to shooting an outlaw or getting shot yourself, which do you figure is better?"

"Shootin' them, I suppose."

"Don't get into no pissin' match with 'em in the first place," said the other.

"If we find rustlers and you try to run, you'll catch a bullet in the back, sure as rain," Slocum said. "I don't miss." He rested his hand on the butt of his Colt Navy. Both men swallowed and nodded. They got the message. Jackson Wimmer had not been quiet about the fight where he had been injured. He might have embroidered his own participation a mite, but he had made it clear that Slocum had been responsible for cutting down the bulk of the outlaws.

"Where we headin'?"

Slocum had pored over a map of the Bar-S for an hour and had located a high pasture that provided most of the forage for the cattle—and which was about perfect for stealing beeves if you were a rustler.

"Follow me," he said, turning his roan's face and heading down toward the road, away from the high meadow. Only when he was sure he was out of sight of the ranch did he veer away from the road and circle westward toward the meadow. The two men with him whispered between themselves. If nothing else, Slocum was forcing them to look at each other as partners rather than foes.

"You recognize him?" Slocum pointed ahead along the winding trail zigzagging higher into the mountains. A lone rider struggled up the steep slope.

"Might be Johnny Stillman."

"He hired on about six weeks back," said the second cowboy. "Came over from Denver, he said, but he didn't know much 'bout the place. Figgered he just rode through. Don't know why he stayed, other than for three squares a day."

Slocum hadn't ordered any of the cowboys to the pasture. The only good reason he could think of why Stillman rode so hard for the meadow was to warn his fellow rustlers. Stillman had always hung back, watching and not saying anything. Slocum had caught him more than once staring hard at him, as if taking his measure. It wasn't so strange for a new foreman to be subjected to such scrutiny, but there had been more in his eyes. Stillman was wondering how good Slocum was with his six-shooter and if maybe Wimmer had brought in a hired gun to stop the rustling.

That was guesswork on Slocum's part, but it fit what he had seen and had felt deep in his gut.

"You think Johnny there's one of the gang rustlin' Bar-S cattle?"

"I'm not accusing him," Slocum said slowly, "but let's say that he's got me wondering what he's up to."

"There! Up there. A lookout's spotted us!"

Slocum had not caught the movement high atop a rocky spire, but the almost drunk cowboy had. He cursed himself for being too wrapped up in his own thoughts. If he intended to stop the rustlers, he had to keep alert.

"Come on, ride like you mean it," Slocum called. He used his reins to whip his roan into a gallop. As he bent forward, he chanced a look behind. He had decided there was a fifty-fifty chance of the two cowboys joining him. It was a good thing he hadn't bet. Both came tearing after him, looking like they were spoiling for a fight.

They got it mighty fast.

The air filled with hot lead all around Slocum as two snipers in the rocks opened up on them. He kept his head down and galloped on, finally leaving the riflemen behind. Both of his cowboys cursed and pissed and moaned, but they stuck with him. He finally reached the top of the long trail and came onto the wide mouth of the lush valley brimming with juicy green grass. Two knots of brown and white cattle grazed nearby. One munched away in peace. The other, maybe fifty head, were being annoyed by two men intent on stealing them.

Slocum headed directly for the rustlers, whooping and shouting as he went. He got within a hundred yards of them before he drew his six-shooter and began firing. At that range, hitting anything was more luck than skill. He got lucky.

One rustler groaned and sagged to the side, falling from his horse. His foot tangled in the stirrup and spooked his mount. The horse lit out like its tail was on fire, dragging the rustler along.

The second rustler had already fled.

Slocum fired a few more times to keep him going, then turned to see how his men were doing. Both had the drop on Johnny Stillman, whose boot had come off and saved him from being dragged to death.

"He confessed, Slocum, he chirped like a bird and said he was guilty. Can we hang him? There's plenty o' trees up here."

"I'm partial to hanging horse thieves," Slocum said, eyeing Stillman closely as he lay stretched out on the ground.

"Not so much cattle thieves. I prefer staking them out in the sun and letting the buzzards pluck out their eyes."

Stillman went pale under his tan. "You can't do that. I got rights. Turn me over to the sheriff."

"The law's a mighty long way off," Slocum said. "The trees are just over there. You prefer getting strung up or staked out?"

"I . . . I'll do whatever you want. Just don't kill me. I got a few dollars." Stillman fumbled in his shirt pocket, tearing it as he pulled out a wad of greenbacks. "Most of a hunnerd dollars."

"Give it to them," Slocum said, pointing to his two cowhands. One reached down and snared the roll of greenbacks with practiced ease. "Count that as your reward for bringing a notorious outlaw to justice," Slocum said to the pair.

They grinned and set about divvying up the money.

"That's a start, but you got to do something else for me," Slocum said, his cold green eyes boring into Stillman's frightened eyes.

"Anything, Slocum, whatever you want."

"Who's the leader of your gang?"

"He . . . George Gilley. He's from down in Texas. I hooked up with him in Santa Fe, been ridin' alongside for close to six months now."

"Six months of rustling, all the way up from New Mexico," Slocum mused. "So you lied about coming from Denver? Doesn't make any difference to me if you rode west or north to get here. You were rustling Bar-S cattle. That's all I care about." Slocum looked hard at Stillman, then shook his head sadly. "All you got to show for it is a hundred dollars, give or take?"

Stillman's head bobbed as if it had been mounted on a spring. He opened his mouth but no words came out.

"I'd say either Gilley is keeping most of the spoils for

himself or you drank up the money mighty fast." Slocum no longer enjoyed toying with Stillman. He had as much information from the rustler as he was likely to get.

"That, whores, some gamblin'," Stillman admitted.

"If you ever want to lie on top of a nickel whore again," Slocum said, "this is what you're going to do. You're going to Gilley and tell him I will string up every last one of his gang when I catch them from now on. If one more cow carrying the Bar-S is lost, I'll come down on his head so hard he'll be sucking wind out of his asshole. You understand?"

"You want him to clear out."

"Don't care if he steals others' cattle," Slocum said. "No more Bar-S cattle get stolen."

"Wh-what about me?"

"He might kill you when you tell him what I just said. If so, he's not likely to believe I mean what I say. There might be a chance he does believe me. I'd highly recommend that you hightail it out of Colorado and find some other line of work you're better suited for."

Stillman's head bounced up and down.

"You got his horse?" Slocum asked.

"Right here, Slocum." One cowboy held up the reins. The boot still dangled from the right stirrup where Stillman's spur had cut into the leather.

"It's property of the Bar-S now. Goes to repay Mr. Wimmer for his losses. That all right with you, Johnny?"

"Yes, sir, it's all right." He had gone pale when Slocum reached across to tap his fingers lightly on the butt of his six-shooter. "You want me to go tell Gilley what you said?"

"Do it," Slocum said. "The boys and me, we got a couple gunmen on the trail leading up here to run down."

"Kin I have my boot back?" He reached for it, but Slocum used his own rein to slap Stillman's hand away.

"Get going or I swear I'll stake you out for the buzzards and coyotes to feast on."

Stillman started walking, then began to run with an uneven gait caused by the lack of one boot. Slocum watched as he went.

"You think them rustlers will hightail it?"

Both cowboys watched Slocum closely.

"Yes," was all Slocum said.

3

Slocum rode into the town of Heavenly, looking around. He had worked for Jackson Wimmer for more than three weeks and this was the first time he had a chance to take a break. There were two saloons in town, both looking mighty inviting to a thirsty cowpoke. But he rode past them and stopped at the general store. He had accounts to settle before getting down to some serious drinking.

He created quite a stir going inside the cool, dim general store. Two women looked up, then turned to each other and began whispering. From the way their eyes boldly returned now and again to stare at him, he knew the subject of their discussion. It wasn't often a stranger came into a town this size, and when he did it was not likely as the new foreman of a big spread.

"Howdy, you must be Mr. Slocum," greeted the proprietor, coming around the counter and thrusting out a hand the size of a small ham. "My name's Gutherie."

"Pleased to make your acquaintance, Mr. Gutherie," Slocum said. "I heard tell some of the boys at the Bar-S had run up a bill."

"You never authorized 'em, I know, but they took plenty of flour and sugar a week back." Gutherie's expression hardened.

"They cut open the bags and rode from one end of town to the other. Turned folks as pale as ghosts by giving everyone a good dusting."

"But mighty sweet, I reckon, if they opened the sugar sacks, too." Slocum turned to the women and touched the brim of his hat. "Not that any in Heavenly need to be any sweeter." This provoked titters from the two. They came to the counter and paid their bills, taking time to look Slocum over more closely. After they left, Slocum got down to business.

"How much of a bill did they run up? My cowboys?"

"More 'n twenty dollars, Mr. Slocum. I—" Gutherie's eyes bugged out when Slocum reached into his vest pocket and pulled out a twenty-dollar gold piece. The tiny coin rang true when he dropped it on the counter.

"I don't cotton much to what they did. I've been keeping a tighter rein on them, and I only found out yesterday what they did. Please accept my apologies and those of Mr. Wimmer."

"That old coot never apologized to no one nohow," Gutherie said. His finger traced the circumference of the tiny coin on the counter. "You payin' fer them mangy cayuses?"

"They work for the Bar-S. We want to keep things friendly. I think the bill for the ranch is a considerable bit more."

"More 'n two hundred dollars."

"We're getting close to selling the herd. You'll get your money then."

"If you got any cattle left," Gutherie said.

"We have plenty now that the rustlers decided to move on."

"What's that? The marshal never said anything 'bout that."

"I came to an agreement with them. About half were from Texas. The rest were Utes off the reservation over in Utah. Convinced George Gilley to send the Indians on their way. After that, it wasn't too hard to get him to move on."

"Can't imagine how you did that. You got a way about you, Mr. Slocum. Don't get me wrong. You might charm the bloomers off the women here in Heavenly, but no rustler worth his salt's gonna just mosey on because you told him to."

"You're wrong," Slocum said. "I doubt I could charm the bloomers off any of the fine, upstanding ladies in town. As to the rustlers, after four of them ended up with ropes around their neck and dangling from oak tree limbs, Gilley got the idea."

"You done something the marshal never could then. So Wimmer's herd is in good condition?"

"With plenty of them left to turn a decent profit."

Gutherie slid the coin off the counter and smiled.

"Good doing business with you, Mr. Slocum. That son of a bitch should've hired you a long time back."

"Then there's no problem getting more flour and sugar?" Slocum almost laughed at the way Gutherie tensed. He went on. "Cookie's out of sugar and he's threatening to use cement in his biscuits. With flour, they're bad enough."

"You needin' any salt pork? A man can get mighty tired of eating nothing but fine beef."

Slocum did laugh at this.

"The day I get tired of steak's the day they put me in the ground. Here's what we need." Slocum pulled the penciled list from his pocket. "I'll pick it up later on. Might send Colorado Pete in to get it."

"Him," grumbled Gutherie. "He's the one what dusted the whole danged town with flour."

"I know," Slocum said. "If you need me, I'll be over at the saloon."

"The Prancing Pony's the best of the lot. Cagney over at the Double Diamond waters his whiskey."

Slocum waited a moment to hear the rest. It came quick enough.

"Not that I have that big a stake in the Prancing Pony's business, mind you. Just a little."

"The Pony it is," Slocum said. He stepped out into the cool Colorado afternoon and took a deep breath. The odors of the town hit him like a hammer blow. Heavenly had fewer than a hundred people, but it was still too crowded for his liking. Some of the reasons it seemed so crowded watched him and batted their long dark eyelashes from across the street. Slocum tipped his hat politely to the ladies—different from the two in the general store—and reflected on how mighty friendly this place was. He didn't have to guess much to know how it had gotten its name. So many pretty young ladies certainly made it Heavenly after doing nothing more than chasing cattle with smelly, cussing, unshaven cowboys as his only human companions.

He walked to the Prancing Pony, trying not to appear in too big a hurry. Ridding the countryside of the rustlers had taken most of his time since becoming foreman. After he found Colorado Pete's stash of whiskey and poured it all out, the cowboys had begun putting in a full day's work. Going without liquor had been hard for them, and it had been hard for Slocum, too. He appreciated a dollop now and then to help his digestion.

He deserved a taste as reward for finally running off George Gilley and his gang of cattle thieves.

Slocum paused in the swinging doors and looked around the Prancing Pony. With a name like Heavenly for the town, he had expected Mormons and their nondrinking ways to have a big influence everywhere. He was wrong. Either that or they adhered to a brand of religion that was exactly what he needed. A large picture of a reclining nude woman with hair so red and tits so big that it made Slocum's teeth ache stretched along the wall behind the bar. Inch-deep sawdust gave the saloon a fragrant smell instead of the usual spilled-beer-and-vomit odor found in most watering holes. The tables were neatly arranged and the chairs had been set in precise locations, waiting for customers.

"Come on in, partner," called the barkeep, a small, waspish man with a mustache so thin that Slocum wondered if he poked out eyes if he got too close with it. "You're the first customer of the afternoon. The rest of the boys'll be in shortly."

Slocum wondered at this camaraderie. What if he preferred to drink alone? That never seemed to occur to the cheerful bartender, who'd already set up a shot glass and poured two fingers of whiskey into it.

"First one's on the house."

"This *is* a right friendly place," Slocum said. "The owner of the general store steered me in this direction. Even if he does own part of the bar, he's to be commended. The Prancing Pony is one mighty fine place."

Slocum lifted the glass in salute, downed the contents, and waited for the kick. Warmth spread throughout his belly, but no kick of nitric acid or gunpowder came. He looked at the empty glass and then at the bottle.

"I'll be switched. That is Kentucky bourbon, like it says on the label. Either that or you made your trade whiskey so smooth that it hardly matters."

"Straight from the vat in Kaintuck," the barkeep bragged.

"You gave me one, now sell me another," Slocum said. He took it into his mouth and rolled it around to savor the texture and flow over his tongue. Swallowing almost seemed a crime, but he committed it anyway.

"Mighty fine."

"You must be the new foreman out at the Bar-S," the barkeep said.

"Word gets around."

"Small town. I heard some of the women cackling like hens that there was a new rooster in the yard. That must be you."

Slocum snorted and shook his head. Seemed the only thing the womenfolk in Heavenly had on their mind was finding a husband.

"Are men that scarce in these parts?"

"Well, not exactly, but the good ones have been run off by the rustlers or left for Denver or the goldfields over in Victor.

Not too many decent ranches around here. The Bar-S is the biggest."

"What about yourself?" Slocum asked. "Don't the ladies find you attractive?"

The barkeep preened, twirling his mustache to even tighter points. When he grinned, he showed even, white teeth under the dark mustache.

"Good of you to say that, but don't go spoutin' it too loud. If my wife ever thought I was lookin' at another woman . . ." The bartender ran his finger across his throat and rolled his eyes.

"Jealous?"

"And mean, but a good woman nonetheless. She's a fine mother to our brood—five kids."

The barkeep rambled on about his family, but Slocum's attention drifted to the nude stretched along the wall and the two women in the general store. They had been decent enough looking, and it had been a long spell since he'd had feminine companionship. He wasn't sure those ladies wanted exactly what he did, though. Looking around, he didn't see any pretty waiter girls or cribs where they might take paying customers. The Prancing Pony was a drinking establishment and nothing more.

"We have a card game or two, but that's all," the barkeep said, as if reading his mind. "In a town where the women outnumber the men, not by much but some, there's no call for a soiled dove. The ones what lit here fluttered away soon enough on their way to Durango or Santa Fe."

Slocum reflected on how different life was in Heavenly compared to other towns he had drifted through. Even in Denver, the number of women was considerably less than that of the men. For whatever reason, Heavenly earned its name. He wasn't the settling-down sort, but a longer stay as foreman of the Bar-S looked mighty appealing.

"Howdy, Doc," called the barkeep. "Come on over. You know Mr. Slocum, don't you?"

The portly doctor came into the bar and dropped his black case on the bar where he could keep an eye on it. He dropped his bowler onto the table and ran both hands through thin gray hair.

"Matter of fact, I do." He thrust out his hand. Slocum shook it. Dr. Gainsborough's grip was strong and the calluses showed he was no stranger to hard work, although he must have been pushing sixty.

"The doc and me talked a while back," Slocum said. "He and his wife were out on the road while I was chasing down some rustlers."

"You and Nora? The three of you? You got along?"

The barkeep's eyes threatened to pop out, making him look like a frog with a mustache.

"No reason why not," Slocum said, wondering at the man's reaction. "I tried to get Doc Gainsborough over to see Wimmer, but it never worked out."

"Jackson is a pigheaded old fool," Gainsborough said. "Wouldn't even let me into the house."

"You and Nora went over and he chased you off?" The bartender swallowed hard and then walked off, shaking his head.

"There something I don't know?" Slocum asked. The barkeep's reaction was peculiar. "Don't you usually make house calls?"

"Me and Nora was returning to town after tending a woman up in the hills. She was all alone and needed some comforting. Gave birth to a baby boy. So, yup, I make house calls."

Slocum frowned. He heard something more in Gainsborough's words, but couldn't figure what it might be.

"You ought to come over to the house sometime when you're in town," Gainsborough said. "Nora fixes up a mean plate of beans." He laughed at this. "She never learned to cook too good, but she's got a powerful lot of other talents."

"Being a nurse," Slocum suggested.

"That, too," Gainsborough said, chuckling. "She's mighty pretty and pretty good in bed."

Slocum tried not to react. It was unusual for a medical man to brag on how good his wife was in bed. But then everything about Doc Gainsborough, Nora Gainsborough, and Heavenly seemed odd.

"Got to go. Nora's not fixing dinner tonight, but we'll be eating in bed, if you catch my drift." Gainsborough slapped Slocum on the shoulder and walked out, whistling. He carried his black bag slung over his shoulder and his bowler tilted at a jaunty angle. Barely had he disappeared than the batwing doors swung inward.

"Seamus, come get yourself a drink," the barkeep called to the newcomer. "You know Mr. Slocum?"

Slocum nodded in the young man's direction. While out tracking outlaws, Slocum had crossed Seamus Murphy's spread. It adjoined the Bar-S and was about a tenth as large. Murphy had not been too accommodating, accusing Slocum of trying to rustle his beeves. It had taken some persuading before the young rancher had let Slocum continue after the actual rustlers.

"I know him. He works for Wimmer."

"Don't get on him like that, Seamus. Mr. Slocum is a right pleasant fellow." The barkeep poured a drink. Murphy cradled it in both hands and knocked it back fast. He choked on it, then set the glass down for another. The bartender silently poured.

"Anybody workin' for that son of a bitch can't be good."

"What's your feud with Wimmer?" Slocum asked. "I haven't been around these parts long enough to know all the details."

"Ask him."

"Wimmer hasn't been too alert since he got shot."

"If he got shot through the heart, that's about the only place where it wouldn't hurt him much. He ain't got a heart."

"Any quarrel you have is with him, not me. Let me buy you a drink."

Seamus glowered, and for a moment Slocum thought he was going to decline. Then he nodded once. The barkeep was quick to fill the rancher's glass.

"To good prices for our herds," Slocum said, lifting his glass.

"I can drink to that," Murphy said. "Don't expect me to drink to Wimmer. Won't do it. Never do it."

"Never ask you to," Slocum allowed.

Seamus finished the drink and left on unsteady legs, never looking back. As he disappeared, the bartender leaned over and whispered, although they were once more alone in the saloon.

"There's been bad blood between him and Wimmer since Seamus took over that dinky spread of his. Truth is, Wimmer's done all he can to drive Seamus off. If Seamus doesn't get top dollar for his herd, he might not make it through the winter. Winters can be fierce here and a lot of feed's needed for the breeders."

"So I've heard," Slocum said. He considered another drink, then decided it was high time for him to collect the goods from Gutherie over at the general store and get on back to the Bar-S. The whiskey had been good, even if the conversation had been peculiar. Small towns kept their secrets close to the vest. Between Seamus Murphy, Doc Gainsborough and his wife, and Jackson Wimmer, there seemed a powerful lot was being hidden. As a newcomer, he wasn't privy to it. Truth was, Slocum wasn't much for gossip, though all this could affect how he did his job on the Bar-S.

"No more? You want me to put that on a tab, Mr. Slocum? You can settle up when you get into town next time."

"That's mighty neighborly of you," Slocum said, fishing in his pocket for a few greenbacks, "but I don't know when that might be. Keeping after the rustlers looks to be a full-time job, along with being foreman."

"Anytime you want, you come on in to the Prancing Pony," the barkeep said. He leafed through the greenbacks, peeled away what he needed, and returned the rest to Slocum.

As he stepped into the street, Slocum heard the heavy pounding of hooves. Colorado Pete Kelso was bent low over his horse, whipping it something fierce until the horse's lathered sides heaved. Slocum wondered if the top hand had galloped the horse all the way from the Bar-S. From the way it staggered, that cruelty wasn't out of the question.

"Slocum, Slocum!" Kelso yanked back savagely on the reins and caused the horse to set all four hooves down hard into the dust so that it skidded several yards.

"What's the all-fired trouble?" Slocum went to the man. He felt the heat boiling off the horse. If it had to walk another ten steps, it would collapse under Kelso.

"Back at the ranch. It's him. Mr. Wimmer!" Kelso was as out of breath as his horse.

"Calm down and tell me what's wrong."

"Slocum, he's dead. Mr. Wimmer's dead."

Slocum stared hard at the seedy man, waiting for the rest of the message to be delivered.

Kelso took a deep gulp of air and blurted, "He's been murdered!"

4

Slocum got back to the Bar-S before Colorado Pete because the top hand's horse had been run into the ground reaching Heavenly. Slocum took the steps leading up into the house three at a time. He stopped on the front porch and frowned. Something struck him as odd, then he realized what it was. The cowboys were going about their business as if nothing had happened.

"Hey, Cookie," Slocum yelled. "Anything wrong around here?"

"Yeah, Slocum, and you know what it is. You fergot to bring back the flour."

Slocum waved off the cook and stared at the door into the house. It was closed. Had Kelso played some kind of joke on him? Slocum knew Kelso was likely to think such a thing would be fun, but he had been too distraught for that. The way he had almost killed his horse told the real story. Nothing might be wrong, but Kelso truly thought Jackson Wimmer was dead, and had ridden his horse into the ground to let Slocum know.

His steps tentative, Slocum went to the door. He started to knock, then opened the door and went inside without announcing himself. The stench in the house hit him like a fist.

32

He started breathing through his mouth, as he had so many times out on the battlefield where the dead had piled up in the hot noonday sun. He knew the scent and this was no joke. Someone had died.

Slocum closed the door behind him and went into the parlor. Nothing appeared out of the ordinary in the small, cluttered room. When he went to Wimmer's office, he found the opposite. Everything was wrong. Jackson Wimmer was sprawled in a chair behind the desk, head lolling at a crazy angle. Blood from the wound in his temple had spattered across the desk in a fan of now dark red.

"You got here fast, Slocum." Behind him, Colorado Pete Kelso was pressing close. The top hand never noticed as Slocum pushed him away. "My horse was so tuckered out I couldn't keep up. See? That's him. Wimmer. He's dead."

"I noticed," Slocum said sarcastically. The expression on Kelso's face was unreadable now. The distress he had shown in town was completely gone. It might have been the ride giving him time to think, or possibly it was knowing somebody else had the responsibility for taking care of Wimmer now. Slocum just couldn't decide what thoughts ran through Kelso's head. Then he shrugged it off. Kelso wasn't the problem.

He studied Wimmer closely, but there was no horror written there on his face, or much of anything else. His features were entirely slack and his eyes were closed. A curious thought crossed Slocum's mind. For the first time since meeting him, Wimmer looked at peace.

"Damn," was all Slocum could think to say.

Everyone on the Bar-S was likely to be on the trail, looking for a new job soon enough. Slocum had never heard Wimmer mention any relatives, and no one seemed likely to take over the operation of the Bar-S. That meant the county was likely to seize the place for taxes.

Slocum ignored that concern for the moment. He was more interested in what had happened. He skirted the pool of blood on the floor around the chair and looked closely at Wimmer. A six-shooter lay on the far edge of the desk, butt away from Wimmer. Leaning over, Slocum pressed his fingers into the dead man's throat. The flesh was cool, but not yet as cold as it would be eventually. There was no pulse beating in the old man's chicken-thin neck, but with the hole in his temple, there wasn't much chance of life persisting. Still, Slocum had to check. Wimmer had proven to be a tough old bastard and might cling to a thread of life, even with so much of his blood spattered across the desk and drained onto the floor.

A roar outside in the yard diverted Slocum's attention. He went to the door and saw Colorado Pete Kelso on the porch addressing the gathered cowboys.

"I recognized the pistol on the floor," Kelso shouted. "It wasn't Mr. Wimmer's."

"Whose was it, Pete?" Whoever shouted from the back of the tight knot of men attracted Slocum's attention. He stepped to one side and tried to see who had asked the question.

"I recognized the six-gun," Kelso said, holding up his open hand to forestall more questions. "It wasn't Mr. Wimmer's, no, sir! It was Seamus Murphy's!"

"How do you know that?" Slocum asked. He craned his neck to get a look at the men at the rear of the crowd. He wanted to know who had set up Kelso to answer a question most of the cowhands weren't likely to ask. Whoever had shouted it out was now moving through the small herd of eleven cowboys.

"I seen him with it in town," said Kelso. "That's Murphy's gun. He musta shot our boss. Murdered him!"

"Why'd he do that?"

Kelso turned on Slocum and glared at him.

"You're new around here, Slocum. Seamus Murphy and Mr. Wimmer have locked horns ever since Murphy started running beeves on his spread a year back. He lets 'em eat Bar-S grass, then brags on it in town. He's even been breedin' his cattle with Mr. Wimmer's prize bull and thinkin' nobody noticed."

"That's true, Slocum," said a man in the front of the crowd. "Murphy took a swing at Wimmer a couple months back. I saw 'im do it outside the Prancing Pony. Ain't no love lost between the pair of them."

"Murphy killed our boss," Kelso said. "What are we gonna do about it?"

"String the Irish bastard up! I'll get a rope!"

The gunshot froze everyone in their tracks. Slocum lowered his Colt Navy and let the muzzle purposefully rove around the gathered cowboys until he had their complete attention.

"Murphy didn't shoot him," Slocum said. "That might be Murphy's six-shooter on the desk. I don't know about that, but I was drinking with Murphy about the time Jackson Wimmer died."

"You was drinkin' with that son of a bitch?" Kelso sounded ugly.

"We were having words," Slocum said. "He's an argumentative cuss, that I'll give him, but we were under the same roof back in town. I don't recall seeing him with iron slung at his side either."

"That's 'cuz he dropped it here when he shot Mr. Wimmer!"

"Why'd he leave it behind?" Slocum knew that logic meant nothing to them. Their boss had been murdered, and they wanted blood. Slocum knew most of them hadn't liked Jackson Wimmer all that much, and doing something about his death would put a dab of balm on their guilty consciences.

"Who knows what goes through a killer's head? He panicked. Is that a good enough reason, Slocum?"

"No, it's not. Murphy was hot under the collar when I talked to him, but he didn't have the look of a man who had murdered anyone and panicked."

"Might be you and him . . ." Kelso's words trickled away

to nothing when he saw the look in Slocum's cold green eyes.

"Go fetch the marshal," Slocum said. "I don't reckon you thought to do that before you rode back."

"He won't care. Him and Wimmer weren't on friendly terms."

"Wimmer wasn't on friendly terms with much of anyone," Slocum said, thinking of what Dr. Gainsborough had said about Wimmer always refusing medical help, no matter how serious it was. Slocum had almost gotten his head bitten off when he suggested that he fetch the doctor to look after Wimmer's gunshot wounds.

"We kin jist bury him," suggested a cowboy. "No need to rile up folks over in Heavenly."

"Get the damned marshal," Slocum said. "Now!"

Kelso jumped a foot, then snaked down the steps and went to get a fresh horse. Slocum waited until Kelso disappeared down the road in a cloud of dust before addressing the mumbling crowd of cowboys.

"You all have work. Get to it."

"Murphy's been a real pain in the ass. We oughta—"

"You oughta do your work and let the law worry about this," Slocum said, drowning out the man's protests. The hands mumbled a few more seconds, then went off in twos and threes arguing over what Wimmer's death meant and what they should do.

Certain that he was not going to be bothered, Slocum went back into the house. The stench staggered him. He opened the windows and left the door standing wide. It was getting cooler as the sun slipped behind the mountains to the west, but inside the house it was still hot enough to bake the dead man's flesh and get it rotting.

Slocum was no expert, but touching Wimmer's throat again convinced him the man had not been dead all that long. He went over all that Seamus Murphy had said to him in the saloon and how long afterward Kelso had arrived with the news. There was no way Murphy could have killed Wimmer. Slocum picked up the six-shooter from the desktop and opened the gate. Slowly turning the cylinder, he saw that a single shot had been fired. He put it back on the desk where he had found it, then looked more closely at Wimmer.

The bullet had gone into Wimmer's right temple and blown most of the left side of his head across the desk. Even if the initial shot had not killed him, the copious blood gushing from the wound had killed him within seconds. Slocum peered at the entry wound and found a ring of unburned gunpowder. The muzzle had been close enough to the man's head to burn some of the wispy white hair there. Slocum had seen men with belly guns cram them into their foe's gut and fire point-blank. The bullets hadn't killed the intended victims, but setting fire to their clothing had.

Murphy's six-gun had been no farther than an inch or two from Wimmer's head when it was fired.

Slocum tried to figure out how this could have happened. Did the murderer threaten him and Wimmer mouth off? An infuriated man might squeeze the trigger and send Wimmer to the Promised Land. If Wimmer and whoever had killed him argued, why wasn't Wimmer shot in the front? And why drop the gun onto the edge of the desk, on the side opposite from Wimmer's head wound?

It didn't make a whole lot of sense.

Slocum pawed through the papers stacked to one side on Wimmer's desk, but saw nothing remarkable there. A few drops of the rancher's blood dotted the papers, but from where Wimmer sprawled in his chair, it was quite possible the blood had spattered this far.

Slocum sank down into the chair opposite the desk and leaned back, staring at Wimmer. He shook his head sadly.

"You crazy old coot. Not a friend in the world and about everyone you ever met turned into an enemy." Slocum leaned back, laced his fingers behind his head, and stared up. For a moment he wasn't sure what he saw. Then he stood and looked closer. He finally climbed to the desktop and examined a hole in the wood ceiling beam.

He pressed his index finger into the hole.

"About .45 size," he decided. "How'd a slug get shot into the ceiling?" He rubbed the area around the hole, pushing away a few splinters. The hole was recent and the wood as yet untouched by air and dust. Whether it had been made today or last week, he couldn't say. With only one bullet fired from the six-shooter, this round was something of a mystery.

He hopped down and prowled about the room, not sure what he was looking for. Something struck him as wrong, but he couldn't put his finger on it. Although he hated to admit it, the situation was pretty much as Kelso had said. Somebody had come in, drawn the six-gun, and killed Jackson Wimmer.

"Using Seamus Murphy's six-gun," Slocum added.

Slocum left the room and went to sit on the porch to wait for the marshal. What had started as a pleasant day had turned ugly mighty fast.

5

"Damn mess," muttered Marshal Zamora as he walked around, carefully avoiding the dried pool of blood soaked into the rug. The portly lawman shook his head in disgust. "Glad I'm not havin' to clean up the blood. The whole damn carpet's probably ruined. Expensive, too."

"You didn't much like him, did you?" Slocum asked.

"You always ask questions you know the answer to, Slocum?" Zamora started to spit, but couldn't find a cuspidor. He went to the window, stuck his head out, and decorated a plant below with a brown gob of chaw. He took his time coming back, pointedly ignoring Wimmer to stare at the gun on the desktop. "That's Seamus Murphy's gun. I remember him waving it around a week or two back. I took it away from him."

"What'd you do with it?"

"Gave it back the next day. Kelso bent my ear the whole way out here about how Murphy's the killer. Got to admit he might be right. That's Murphy's piece."

"I was in the Prancing Pony with Murphy about the time this happened," Slocum said.

"Time's a crazy thing when you're drinking. Downright loco," the marshal said, finally pushing his hat back on his forehead and taking his bandanna to wipe away sweat. When he finished that chore, he dabbed at a drop of tobacco at the corner of his mouth. "Damn hot in here. Not a breeze blowing outside to get rid of the heat." Zamora coughed. "Or the stench. Damn, but he's stinking up the place."

"What are you going to do?" Slocum watched Zamora turn Murphy's six-gun over and over in his hands, looking at it from every possible angle as if it might give him some clue not obvious to a casual observer. He finally tucked it into his belt when nothing new came to him.

"Need to find the bullet that blew out Wimmer's brains," Zamora said. "That about finishes what I can do here."

"He didn't go far from where he's sitting," Slocum said.

"Think he might have been standing when he was shot and then fell into the chair?" Zamora looked at the chair legs.

"Doesn't look like it. If he fell back that hard, the chair would have tipped over," Slocum said. "Besides, he's behind the desk. Mighty hard for him to move around. When I found him, his legs were up underneath, as if he was sitting when he was shot."

"Or flat out collapsed. This rung's loose and the back leg's cracked." Marshal Zamora pressed down on the straight back of the chair and it suddenly collapsed, sending Wimmer heavily to the floor. Zamora jumped away in surprise.

"You figured that out pretty good, Marshal," Slocum said. "He was already sitting down." Slocum came over and sighted along an imaginary line where Wimmer's head would have been. Even turning a little after being shot, the bullet wouldn't have gone far. Slocum looked back at the bullet hole in the ceiling. There was no way Wimmer could have been in the chair and had the bullet end up in the wood beam. Before Slocum could ask the marshal about this, Zamora let out a yelp of victory.

"Got it." Zamora drew a knife from a sheath at his belt and worried away at a cabinet. From the wood he dug out a slug and held it up. "Can't say for sure, but it looks like it's got blood on it."

"It went into the wood at about the right level if Wimmer was sitting down when he was shot, too," Slocum said. He stepped off the distance. The bullet had bored its way into the cabinet only six feet from the body.

"That's all I need from here." Zamora matched the slug with the bore of Murphy's six-shooter. "It fits."

"There are close to a dozen men here at the ranch who might have shot him," Slocum said. "But none of the cowboys even heard the shot."

"I talked to a few of them. As loco as it sounds to me, they were actually working. You whipped 'em into shape, Slocum. I'll give you that."

"They knew which side of the bread their butter was on," Slocum said. "Nobody on the Bar-S profited from Wimmer's death."

"Most all of them hated his guts, but you're right," Zamora said. "I know men like your cowboys. If any of them had plugged Wimmer, they'd be in California by now."

"What do you do now?"

"Reckon someone could have sneaked in and put this slug into his head who wasn't Seamus Murphy," the marshal said. He said the words, but did not harbor any doubt that Murphy had been the gunman. "I'll hie on back to town and ask some questions."

From the way Marshal Zamora held the six-shooter responsible for the killing, Slocum knew what that meant.

"Murphy?"

"Have to ask how his gun came to be the murder weapon," Zamora said. "You don't think he did it?"

"I already said I was with him about the time Wimmer was killed. His alibi can't get much better than that."

"I'll still need to find out why him and his six-gun weren't together," Zamora said.

"I'll ride with you."

Zamora looked a bit sour at this, but said nothing as he left. Slocum mounted and rode alongside the lawman, but there wasn't much talking all the way into Heavenly. Both were lost in their own thoughts, but Slocum's kept rolling in big circles like a wheel without getting anywhere.

Zamora dismounted in front of the tumbledown shack that served as the town jail. From its condition, Slocum guessed there wasn't much call to lock up the citizens of Heavenly.

"I saw him at the saloon when I passed by," the marshal said. "You can come along but keep your tater trap shut. Understand, Slocum?"

"All right," he said, trailing the marshal to the Prancing Pony. Zamora hitched up his gun belt and went in, not bothering to see if Slocum followed.

Slocum edged into the saloon in time to see Zamora bump up against Seamus Murphy, forcing the young rancher back against the bar. The marshal's considerable belly held Murphy in place when he tried to slide first one way and then the other.

"I got questions," Zamora said.

"I didn't do anything," Murphy said, his words slurred from too much booze. The owner of the general store and bar stood at the far end, watching what went on. Slocum looked around for the regular barkeep, but didn't see him. Gutherie obviously looked after his interests in the bar by working here if things got slow at the general store.

"How'd your gun get out at the Bar-S then?"

"I lost it. Maybe it was stolen. I don't wear it much and keep it hung on a peg near my front door. Anybody could have swiped it."

"And who might that have been?"

Zamora glared at Murphy while he kept him pinned against the bar.

"How should I know? Maybe it was Wimmer. He hates me."

"And you hate him, don't you?" The lawman was coming to a decision Slocum didn't like. For whatever reason, Murphy didn't see what it was.

"I hated him as much as he did me."

"I think you plugged him, got scared at what you'd done, dropped yer six-shooter, and hightailed it back to town to pretend nothing had happened."

"He's not that good an actor, Marshal," Slocum said.

"Why are you sticking up for him?"

"I don't have a dog in this fight. I just don't see any way he could have killed Wimmer and ridden into town so close to the time Wimmer was killed." Slocum looked hard into Murphy's bloodshot eyes. The man was on the point of passing out from too much whiskey. He might be trying to drown his guilt, but Slocum thought the binge was due to something else. "You leave your horse at the town livery?"

"I don't have money enough for that," said Murphy.

"Then there'd be about everyone in town seeing that his horse was lathered from galloping here so fast. When Kelso came to tell me, he damn near killed his horse pushing it all the way from the Bar-S. Wimmer hadn't been dead more than an hour when Kelso left the ranch to tell me."

"I'll ask around," Zamora said. He backed off, letting Murphy breathe a little easier. The respite did nothing to stop the young rancher's smoldering anger.

"You hate me, just like Wimmer did. You all do. Every damn one of you in town hates me."

"Not much to like, is there?" With that, Zamora swung around and left.

"You got a reason for tying one on?" Slocum asked when the marshal was gone.

"I feel like it. What's it to you, Slocum? You think you can do Wimmer's dirty work for him and steal my ranch and cattle? I'm not going to give up that easy."

"Wimmer's dead. Are you so soused you didn't hear what the marshal said?"

"Yeah, right, he's dead. Between the ears. And in the heart. The man isn't even human."

Murphy tried to catch himself against the bar and missed, landing heavily on the sawdust-covered floor.

"He's drunker than I thought," Gutherie said, peering over the top of the bar. "He told me to cut him off when he ran though the ten dollars he dropped on the bar. Reckon I ought to stop settin' drinks in front of him?"

"He drink it all up?"

"Yeah, surely did," the bar owner said. He looked at Slocum and nervously wiped at his lips. "You think he killed Wimmer?"

"I told the marshal I didn't think so. He was in here about the time Wimmer was killed. Your barkeep can back me up on that. You think Murphy can be in two places at once?"

"Well, I dunno," Gutherie said. "No good askin' after Bennett. He lit out with Lulu Garston. Left his wife and five young 'uns." Gutherie looked puzzled. "Why he'd leave with a woman like that is beyond me."

"Might be he got tired of his wife and brood," Slocum said, not caring one whit about that. He remembered how the barkeep had said his wife was stepped-on-rattler mean. "When was the last time you saw Murphy?"

"I been tryin' to remember if I saw him wearin' his six-gun when he came into town earlier. Can't rightly say, one way or the other. He might have been packin' then."

"He wasn't," Slocum said. He stared at Murphy, heaped up on the floor. There was no reason for Slocum to get more involved than he already was. "To hell with it," he said, bending down and getting his arm around Murphy. He heaved and pulled the rancher to his feet. Murphy grumbled and cursed the whole way outside into the cool afternoon wind blowing down from the north.

"There's the varmint! Lynch him!"

For an instant, Slocum thought the men from the Bar-S had come to town and picked up their refrain again. Then he saw a dozen of the Heavenly townsfolk shaking their fists at Murphy and working themselves up into a killing rage.

"Hold on," Slocum said, dropping Murphy into a chair on the boardwalk. He started to slide out. Slocum grabbed him by the collar and pulled him upright. "Does it look like he's in any condition to kill anybody?"

"He's in plenty good condition to swing for killin' Jackson Wimmer!"

Another in the crowd shouted, "He's drunk so he won't have to face hisself. That means he's guilty as sin!"

"It means he's drunk," Slocum said, stepping between Murphy and the crowd. "He was with me in the saloon when Wimmer was shot. From all I can tell, he never left, and got himself likkered up till he can't see straight."

"The marshal said his gun killed Wimmer."

"That doesn't mean *he* killed my boss," Slocum said. Logic meant nothing to the crowd. Zamora had not been too politic about asking after Murphy's whereabouts and had given them the idea there was only one suspect—the man whose gun had killed Jackson Wimmer.

Slocum considered which of the men to shoot first if it came to that—he was not going to turn Murphy over to a lynch mob, even if he had thought the man was guilty.

A couple of men in the front saw the resolve in his eyes and the steadiness of his hand resting on his six-shooter. They backed up into the crowd and created enough of a disturbance that the rest of the men began thinking of other things. When they did, the mob began to dissolve into individuals, and Slocum saw that the threat was over for the moment.

"Go on about what you're doing. Go into the Prancing Pony. Gutherie's got plenty of good booze in there waiting for you. Or go home. Just go somewhere else."

A few grumbled but the crowd dispersed, leaving Slocum with a very drunk Seamus Murphy. The rancher muttered and thrashed about, fighting unseen demons in his stupor. Slocum grabbed him by the collar and heaved him to his feet. Murphy stumbled and went forward. Slocum did nothing to slow his progress over the railing and into the watering trough. Two horses reared and tried to pull away as the man splashed into the water.

"Wh-whatsit?"

"Go home," Slocum said.

"Who're you to dunk me like that?" Murphy tried to get out of the trough and fell back. Only then did he realize he was sober enough to complain and still too drunk to do anything about it. "Help me out, will you?"

Slocum grabbed the young man's arm and pulled, getting him to his feet in the street. Murphy dripped water and created a tiny mud puddle around him.

"You stood up for me, didn't you, Slocum?"

"Let everyone in town cool off. Not a one of them even liked Jackson Wimmer, but all of them were willing to string you up."

"I'm glad he's dead," Murphy said.

"I don't much care if that's the liquor talking or some truth boiling up from your miserable soul. Shut your mouth and go about your business. Marshal Zamora will figure out what happened."

"I didn't kill him."

"I know," Slocum said. But in spite of all he said, he was beginning to wonder if Murphy might somehow have plugged Wimmer, then made it into town to argue with him. He shook his head. It didn't seem possible.

But as he watched Murphy stumble off, his gait uneven from too much whiskey and his cursing of Jackson Wimmer slurred, Slocum had to wonder if Kelso and Zamora and the rest of the town might not be right.

6

"Pleasant day for a plantin'," Colorado Pete Kelso said.

"No day's a good day to be buried if you're the one going six feet under," Slocum said. He wished Kelso would ride with the rest of the cowboys from the Bar-S and not bedevil him with his observations on life and mortality.

"Fer Wimmer, it's a good day. Fer us, it is, too. I never cottoned much to the way he treated me. I'm surprised you got along so well with him, Slocum. You look to have a nasty temper."

"I understood him," Slocum said.

"How's that?"

Slocum looked at Kelso and silenced the man. He'd had enough of the endless rambling. He hated going to funerals and, even more so, hated attending this one. Nobody in Heavenly had much liked Wimmer, but Slocum had gotten along with him because he refused to take any guff off the old man. There had been a grudging admiration between them that could never have blossomed into friendship, not that it mattered now. Wimmer was dead and, as foreman of the Bar-S, Slocum was responsible for seeing that the funeral went smoothly. That it took every last penny he had been paid during his stint as foreman on the Bar-S mattered

47

less to Slocum than having to listen to some preacher's platitudes about Wimmer going to a better place.

As they rode toward the small cemetery on the far side of Heavenly, Slocum saw a small knot of people already gathered inside the knee-high stone-walled enclosure. Off to one side stood Marshal Zamora, arms crossed and his big belly jutting out over his broad, hand-tooled gun belt. Standing at the grave was the preacher, nervously flipping through pages in his Bible, probably trying to find a passage that summed up what a son of a bitch Wimmer was without actually saying so. Slocum was moderately surprised to see Gutherie in the small crowd of other merchants. They talked with much waving of arms and hand motions to the undertaker.

Slocum tried to remember the man's name and couldn't. That might have come from his distaste of funerals, or the fact that the undertaker didn't have much of a personality. All he'd done was nod, smile, and write down whatever Slocum said. He might not have said more than a dozen words, and those were all insincere, practiced words of sympathy. Slocum would have admired him more if he had come right out and said what he thought of Wimmer. After all, there was no family to coddle or friends to insult.

Slocum pointed to the side of the cemetery outside the wall where the Bar-S hands could leave their mounts. Some of them would have ridden right up to the grave, their horses' hooves digging at the other graves. For all that, some of the cowboys would have downed a pint of Gutherie's whiskey, then pissed on Wimmer's pinewood coffin.

"Shall we begin, Mr. Slocum?" The unctuous undertaker folded his hands in front of him. "The day's turning mighty hot, and I'm certain you don't want folks to get heat stroke."

"Do you?"

"What?" The question took the undertaker by surprise. "I don't understand what you mean."

"If some folks keeled over from heat stroke, they might die and you'd get that much more business."

"I take it that you don't want pictures," the man said, dropping his oily tone and glaring at Slocum.

"Not of the corpse, not of the people here, not of anything," he said. Slocum motioned for the cowboys to gather around the grave. It took several seconds for them all to realize they ought to remove their hats. Only when they had did Slocum give the preacher the signal to begin the service.

Slocum's attention began to drift when the preacher got to the part about "I am the resurrection and the life." Slocum looked around and wondered who the nattily dressed man crowded close to the marshal was. He wore a tie with a headlight diamond the size preferred by tinhorn gamblers, a jacket of fine linen, and tiny eyeglasses that pinched down on his nose. There was no hint of watery eyes peering through those lenses, though. His blue eyes were bright and sharp and fixed on Slocum like a hawk might examine a rabbit on the run.

Soon enough, the service ended and the preacher gave the undertaker the signal to begin shoveling dirt into the grave and on top of Wimmer's coffin. Every spadeful of dirt echoed and made Slocum wince just a little. He turned and told the cowboys, "Take the rest of the day off. There's no need to get back to the ranch before dawn, but you'd better not be so hungover you can't do a day's work tomorrow."

They let out a whoop and tore off for the two saloons. Gutherie grinned at Slocum, tipped his hat, and hurried off. He had customers to get drunk.

"Mr. Slocum, I'd like a word with you. And with Mr. Kelso also." The well-dressed man's manner was brusque and all business. That suited Slocum just fine. He wanted to partake of some of Gutherie's whiskey and get the taste of dirt and death out of his mouth.

"This here's Mr. Longmont," the marshal said. "He's the only attorney in town."

"Must make for a hard life, having to sue yourself all the time."

"I always win in court that way, Mr. Slocum."

"Seems like the opposite would be true, too."

"Please come to my office for the reading of the will. I want Mr. Kelso to hear it, too."

"Will?"

"Mr. Wimmer's. You knew that he had registered a new will only last week, didn't you?"

"I didn't know he had an old will, much less a new one," Slocum said. "Don't make no never-mind to me, one way or the other." He rubbed dust off his lips. The ride into Heavenly had been a dry one, and standing around in the late summer sun had worn him down, just as the undertaker had predicted. An entire bottle of whiskey from behind the bar would suit him just fine, and Longmont was keeping him from it.

"Better do it, Slocum." Marshal Zamora fixed him with a cold stare.

"Come on, Pete. The sooner they have their say, the sooner we can drink."

Colorado Pete grumbled, but followed along behind. Slocum set the pace just a little faster than Longmont or Zamora could keep up with. He wasn't sure where the lawyer's office was, but Heavenly wasn't big enough for there to be many places to hide it.

When he saw Doc Gainsborough and his wife, Nora, down the main street, he headed for them. His instincts were right because the sign over the door behind the doctor verified that this was the lawyer's office.

"They got us all rounded up, I reckon," Gainsborough said.

"You weren't at the funeral," Slocum said. "Don't like seeing a patient put underground?"

"Jackson was hardly Ben's patient. That old galoot refused all treatment, though it was offered more than once," Nora Gainsborough said tartly. She started to continue her defense of her husband and his doctoring skills as Longmont came up, key in hand. He pushed past them and opened the office door.

"Please, come in. I hope I have set out enough chairs."

"I kin stand," Kelso said. Slocum wished he had spoken up first. If he stood near the door, he could be the first out and on the way to the Prancing Pony Saloon when the lawyer was done with his speechifying.

Slocum found himself seated across the huge oak desk from the lawyer, with Ben Gainsborough and his wife to his right. To his left, Marshal Zamora shifted restlessly in the straight-backed wooden chair.

"Mr. Wimmer made a new will shortly after you became Bar-S foreman, Mr. Slocum." Longmont cut open an envelope that had been sealed with wax. He spread it out on the table in front of him. "I certify that this is a legal document, duly witnessed and executed by Jackson Wimmer's hand and of his own free will."

"Get on with it, will you, Longmont?" Marshal Zamora was as antsy as Slocum, but the lawman appeared to know what was coming.

"The Bar-S is a prosperous ranch and worth a hundred thousand dollars, more or less."

Slocum nodded. He wasn't the sort to tally up values like that, but the extent of the land and the number of cattle running on the range were easily worth that amount. If he had to put a value on it all, he might have guessed it was worth even more. With attention to actually running the ranch, it could be twice as prosperous in a few years.

"There's a lot of legal mumbo jumbo, but it all comes down to this. Wimmer left the Bar-S to you, Mr. Slocum. In its entirety."

Nora Gainsborough shot to her feet and stormed out of the office. Ben Gainsborough clapped Slocum on the shoulder and said, "Congratulations. This makes you a rich man, Mr. Slocum." He quickly followed his wife from the office.

Marshal Zamora left without uttering a word. Colorado Pete Kelso simply said, "Shit."

Slocum had to agree with the top hand.

His top hand.

7

John Slocum stood on the porch of the ranch house and stared into the sunrise. He had returned from Heavenly having had only two shots of whiskey all night long. He had moved his gear from the bunkhouse into the house and stared at Wimmer's bed when he got back ahead of all the ranch hands. He could have taken the mattress and fine Irish linen off the bed and replaced them so he wouldn't be sleeping in a dead man's bed. Instead, he had paced around the house, avoiding the office where Wimmer had died, and eventually settled on the porch. He had watched the stars fade away as the sun rose, and then simply stared at the new day.

"New day," he mused. "What do I do with a ranch?"

Slocum spoke aloud as if expecting an answer—and he heard the voice deep within saying this might be his last, best chance to settle down. Heavenly was filled with lovely ladies. He was the most prominent rancher throughout the area now, with holdings making him unbelievably wealthy. That he had done nothing to earn it rankled, though. Wimmer must have known Slocum would worry over that. It was one thing to put in a day's work as foreman and earn his keep. It was another having it all handed to him on a silver platter held by a dead man's hand.

But the trail got lonely year after year, and settling down had its benefits. His parents had been content all their lives at Slocum's Stand, up until they had died while he was away at war. He had returned and been the sole owner. Slocum touched the watch in his vest pocket. That was the only legacy his brother Robert had left him. He had always assumed the two of them would split the family farm and live out their lives after the war.

Robert had died during Pickett's Charge, and Slocum had returned to recuperate after getting gut-shot by Bloody Bill Anderson for questioning how their commander, William Quantrill, had ordered every male of fighting age slaughtered in the Lawrence, Kansas, raid. He had needed quiet to regain his strength, but a carpetbagger judge had taken a shine to the farm and wanted to raise thoroughbreds on it. No taxes paid during the war, he had lied. Forged documents backed up the demand. Pay up or get out.

When the judge had shown up at Slocum's Stand with a hired gun to enforce the eviction notice, the man had indeed taken ownership of the farm, but not the way he'd intended. Slocum had left two fresh graves by the springhouse and had ridden west without so much as a backward look. The wanted poster on him for killing a federal judge, even a corrupt one, had dogged his trail for years.

The Bar-S was his chance to settle down and become part of a community that would not care about a Reconstruction judge's death so many years earlier.

"Mine," he said, looking at the land now lighting up with warmth as the sun rose. All that the sun touched in his sight was his because a cranky old coot had bequeathed it to him.

But it wasn't his. He had done nothing to earn it. Running off a gang of rustlers hardly counted as enough of a deed to merit the Bar-S as a reward.

He'd sell the ranch, split the money equally with all the cowboys, and then move on. It was the right thing to do.

"Slocum, I want a word with you."

"What is it, Kelso?" Slocum saw how Colorado Pete's gait was a bit unsteady. He and the rest of the hands from the Bar-S had about drunk the Prancing Pony dry, and it still showed.

"I want a cut."

"What are you talking about?"

"The ranch. The goddamn ranch! You don't deserve to git it all. I want a share. A big one. I been here for two years and you ain't even worked the range for two months."

Slocum said nothing and let the man rant on. It was true he had been at the Bar-S for a short time, but he had run off the rustlers. Slocum wasn't sure Kelso had ever tried. The man lacked the spine for such a chore.

"Might be you ought to split it with me right down the middle, you and me partners," Kelso said.

"What about the rest of the hands?"

"What about 'em? This is somethin' me and you have to thrash out."

"Don't start thrashing, Kelso," Slocum said softly. "You won't like the way that turns out."

"You can't git the whole damned ranch and not let me have some of it. Ten thousand dollars. That sounds fair. The Bar-S is worth a hell of a lot more 'n that."

"What'll you do if I don't give you a cut? Quit?"

"Gimme what I'm askin' for or you'll regret it!"

Slocum paused as he stared into Kelso's bloodshot eyes. A smile curled his lips. It wasn't a friendly smile.

"I'd regret it if I gave you more than your salary. Truth is, I regret giving you that much since you don't do much to earn it."

"I'm top hand here! I—"

"Mr. Slocum! Mr. Slocum! We got big trouble!" A young cowboy stumbled up, out of breath. "Me 'n Jenks was up in the high meadow countin' steers. They're back. They came back!"

"The steers? What are you sayin'?" Colorado Pete turned

too fast and almost lost his balance. Slocum knew if he had been a step or two closer, he could have heard the liquor sloshing around in the top hand's belly.

"Shut up, Kelso. Ryan's trying to say that the rustlers are working our herd again." Slocum fixed his cold stare on Kelso. "The rustlers are stealing *my* cattle. You have a problem with that?"

Pete Kelso looked confused. He started to speak, and then clamped his mouth shut.

"Good. Ryan, get a half dozen men who can ride without falling out of the saddle and be sure they've all got rifles. Be here in the yard—*my* yard—in ten minutes. We're going to get ourselves some scalps. Rustlers' scalps."

"Yes, sir!" Ryan dashed off, leaving Kelso behind.

"You still working for the Bar-S or are you going to pack your gear and leave? Your choice, Kelso. I want you to have made it by the time I get back."

"You ain't doin' me out of a good job, Slocum, any more 'n you can do me outta my share of the Bar-S."

"Then ride with me while we're hunting down the outlaws. I don't want to lose one more steer to rustlers."

Kelso walked off, grumbling. Slocum fingered his six-shooter, considering how easy putting a slug into the man's back would be to end all the bickering. He had decided to sell the Bar-S and split the money among the cowboys until Kelso had demanded a share. Running a going concern like this ranch wouldn't be all that hard, and settling down might not be such a bad idea. Succeeding at running the ranch would spite Colorado Pete Kelso.

Slocum ducked into the house, found a rifle with ammunition, and then went to saddle his roan. It was time to start defending Bar-S property. *His* property.

"They was o'er yonder," Ryan said, standing in the stirrups and pointing across the grassy valley. "Jenks, he saw 'em cuttin' out a dozen head and herdin' 'em up the far side."

Slocum sat stock-still as he listened and watched and considered where the rustlers might have taken the stolen beeves. Where Ryan pointed wasn't their likely destination. The canyon walls rose sharply not a mile beyond. Unless the cattle thieves had found a pass through the mountains, there was no way of driving the cattle much farther. More likely, they had headed due north with the small herd, thinking to get out of the valley to sell it in North Park. The few days on the trail would give them plenty of time to run the Bar-S brand.

"What you thinkin' on, Mr. Slocum?" Ryan's eagerness was matched by that of his partner, Jenks.

"Which way would they go?" Slocum said aloud as he worked out the trail in his mind and the best way of catching the rustlers.

"It'd be like he said, Slocum," Kelso piped up. "They'd head due west."

"You know a way out of the valley and over the mountain?"

"Well, there's got to be one. Sure, there's one over there," Kelso said, arm waving vaguely in the direction of the towering hills.

"They went north," Slocum said. "Kelso, you and Jenks find where they rounded up the cattle and follow the trail. North."

"And me, Mr. Slocum? What about me?" Ryan asked.

"We'll cut across the valley and try to head them off," Slocum said. He wished Ryan had roused a couple more men from their liquor-induced stupor. Even if there were only a handful of rustlers, two men fighting them would be a chore. Depending on Kelso for any help was out of the question, but he didn't want to send the top hand off by himself to get into any mischief. While he didn't know Jenks as well as he did Ryan, he thought the young cowboy would keep Kelso honest. Or as honest as possible.

"What if we come up on 'em?" Jenks sounded eager for a fight.

"Wait for us to come in from the other side. More likely, we'll find them first. You come running when you hear gunfire," Slocum said. "Now you and Kelso get moving. I don't want to track them varmints in the dark."

Jenks and Kelso rode away at a brisk trot. Slocum settled his hat and made some guesses as to how far and how fast the rustlers might have traveled. Then he took off at a gallop, Ryan close behind.

As he rode, Slocum called out to Ryan, "How did you decide to come up here? Weren't you and Jenks celebrating?"

"Truth is, Mr. Slocum, neither me nor Jenks drinks."

"Didn't find yourselves a filly or two for celebrating with?"

"That wouldn't be right either, not till I get married. It's ag'in my religion."

"Glad you decided to look after the cattle. You probably saved me losing a hundred head or more."

"We're just doin' our job, Mr. Slocum."

By the time his roan began to flag, Slocum saw the trail leading northward. He drew rein and dismounted, studying the ground carefully. His finger traced out a hoofprint.

"They came from the north sometime last night, but they haven't come back this way. We got in front of them."

"Then we got 'em," Ryan said eagerly. He drew his rifle from the saddle sheath and cocked it. "What are we waitin' for? Let's git 'em!"

"Settle down," Slocum said, getting back into the saddle. "Our horses are tuckered out. We'll walk them for a spell. Keep a sharp eye out for the cattle. Might be the rustlers are having problems with them."

"They're only cows," Ryan said.

"After I ran off Gilley, what remained might not be as good when it comes to rustling," Slocum said. He had swapped stories with others around Heavenly, and had come to the conclusion whoever was rustling from their herds now was likely more comfortable robbing a stagecoach than stealing beeves.

"I hear 'em!"

"Quiet," Slocum said. He heard the lowing cattle, too. The faint puff of wind wouldn't carry sound far. That meant the rustlers were less than a half mile off, probably working the herd up through a stand of pines.

"What do we do, Mr. Slocum?"

"Keep your rifle ready and let's go." Slocum pulled his own rifle out and laid it across the crook of his left arm as he rode. He brought the rifle up and aimed the instant he saw two heifers pop out of the wooded area.

"Where're the rustlers? All I see are them cows."

Slocum waited as he sighted down the barrel of his rifle. At this range, he could choose which eye he wanted to shoot out of a rustler. But nobody rode after the twenty head of cattle that eventually meandered from the woods and stopped to graze on a juicy patch of grass.

"I wasn't wrong. Me and Jenks, we saw men stealin' them cows, Mr. Slocum. I swear it." Ryan sounded so insistent that Slocum had to believe him.

"How many men did you see?"

"Not more 'n four or five. It was hard to tell, but there was more 'n me and Jenks wanted to handle on our own. We're not cowards. We—"

"You did the right thing," Slocum said, cutting him off. He waved Ryan ahead toward the left side of the herd while he circled around the right. The cattle looked up incuriously, then went back to their afternoon snack. Slocum reached the rear of the herd before gesturing for Ryan to join him.

"You stay with the cattle. I'll backtrack."

"You think Jenks and Mr. Kelso already got 'em?"

Slocum wasn't sure what to think. The rustlers had simply abandoned twenty head of cattle for no good reason. There hadn't been any gunfire to signal a tussle between the Bar-S cowboys and the outlaws, but Slocum had to find out for sure.

"If I'm not back in an hour, come looking for me," Slocum said. "Do it quietlike."

"What if I hear shootin'?"

"Stay put. You might drive the cattle back out into the center of the valley where we can keep a better watch on them. Otherwise, you stick close to them."

Slocum plunged into the dark, cool stand of pines and followed the winding trail. The lack of light made it hard to see the hoofprints in the dirt, which was littered with pine needles. He wanted to find the spot where the rustlers had stopped herding and had lit out.

On the far side of the copse, he drew rein when he saw two mounted men a quarter mile off, face-to-face and arguing. Their words got swallowed by distance, but the way they gestured told him this was not a friendly meeting. Slocum pulled his field glasses from his saddlebags and trained them on the men.

He recognized Colorado Pete Kelso right away. The man he argued with had his face turned so Slocum couldn't get a good look, but from the condition of his clothing, he had been on the trail for a long time. Just as Slocum thought he would finally see the unknown man's face, the rider trotted away and rounded a bend in the trail that took him out of sight.

Slocum tucked his field glasses away and faded back into the forest, finding a spot a few yards off the trail to sit and wait as Kelso rode toward him. The top hand passed within ten feet without noticing him. Slocum started to follow, then changed direction and rode back down the trail. Kelso wasn't going to cause any trouble, but the mysterious man he had argued with just might. Until he found where Jenks had gone, Slocum wanted to keep in the shadows as much as possible.

He reached the spot where Kelso and the other rider had exchanged their heated words. A quick look at the ground all torn up by horses' hooves told Slocum they had been here far longer than he had watched. He used his reins to switch his roan into a trot. It was dangerous riding a trail with as many bends and blind twists in it, but an urgency built in his gut.

If he caught the man Kelso had talked to, answers might come pouring out.

He had barely ridden another quarter mile when he saw a horse drinking from a brook running near the trail. He rode over to it and saw blood on the saddle. Slocum thought this nondescript nag was Jenks's horse, but he couldn't be sure, until he pawed through the saddlebags and found a letter addressed to the cowboy.

Slocum reached down, snared the horse's reins, and tugged the nag away from the stream before it bloated. Pulling hard on the reins until it trotted easily on its own accord, Slocum continued back down the trail, more alert than ever. The unknown rider could not have done anything to Jenks without Slocum hearing. That meant whatever had happened to the young cowboy had taken place earlier, maybe right after he and Kelso started on this trail.

"Ohhh," came the moan. Slocum turned, his rifle swinging around. The sound came again, this time accompanied by rustling in some undergrowth near the trail. He dismounted and advanced slowly, alert for a trap. All he found was Jenks, on hands and knees, his bare head caked with blood. Slocum knelt and pulled the cowboy around so he sat on the ground.

"What happened?"

Jenks had a hard time focusing his eyes. Slocum saw that the pupils were different sizes, showing how hard the man had been hit on the head. With gentle probing, he found a two-inch-long gash in the back of the man's head. The size matched pretty well with a pistol barrel.

"Slugged. From behind. Tried to . . . I don't remember what I tried to do. Mr. Slocum?" Jenks collapsed. Slocum let him fall to the ground so he could listen for the other rider. Wherever the rustlers had gone, they must have passed Jenks—or Kelso.

Without a word, Slocum got his arm around the cowboy and got him to his feet. Jenks struggled to walk. Seeing that Jenks would never be able to ride without tumbling from the saddle, Slocum heaved him up and over his horse belly-down.

He looked like a sack of meal, but he proved harder to lash into place. There wasn't any easy way to throw a diamond hitch on the young cowboy to keep him from falling off.

Slocum decided to let the man Kelso had argued with ride on so he could get Jenks cared for. He turned north and led Jenks's horse with its burden back to where Ryan and Kelso circled the milling cattle.

"Mr. Slocum!" Ryan called. "Is he all right?"

"Got clobbered from behind. Otherwise, he's in good enough shape," Slocum said.

"Who hit him?"

Slocum looked hard at Kelso.

"Who was it, Kelso? Who hit Jenks?"

"How should I know? We started out together, but he rode off. Never said a word to me what he was doin'. Just lit out like he had a wild hair up his ass."

Slocum considered asking about the man Kelso had argued with, then decided that it was better to stay quiet on this. For the moment. It might have been only a pilgrim passing through, but it was more likely one of the rustlers.

"You didn't see any trace of them? The rustlers?" Slocum asked.

"Nary a trace," Ryan said. "Is he gonna be all right? Jenks is lookin' kinda pale."

"Why don't you and Kelso get him into town and let Doc Gainsborough poke and prod him some?"

"What are you gonna do, Slocum?" Kelso was not—quite—belligerent.

"The rustlers got off somewhere. I'm going to try to track them down."

"That's mighty dangerous, Mr. Slocum, doin' it all alone. I kin git Jenks into town by myself. You and Mr. Kelso can—"

"Better hurry," Slocum said to Ryan. "Your partner's not going to heal draped over the saddle like that."

"Yes, sir," Ryan said. He was more concerned with his friend than anything else. But Colorado Pete Kelso kept glaring at Slocum, until he finally wheeled his horse around and trotted after Ryan and Jenks.

Slocum waited awhile, then set off after the three men. Finding the rustlers would do him no good. There was nothing to prove they had ever tried to steal any Bar-S cattle, and he had no stomach for going up against an entire gang of rustlers.

But he did want to know what Kelso did once he thought he was out of sight. Slocum left behind the cattle as they grazed, knowing they would find their way to water eventually, where they could be rounded up and moved back into the main herd. As he rode, he wondered about Kelso and how Jenks had come to be laid up the way he was.

The answer seemed obvious.

8

It was well past sundown when Ryan and Kelso got the injured cowboy to Heavenly. Slocum wanted to ride up then and tell Doc Gainsborough that he would see to the bill, but Colorado Pete veered away from the doctor's office and rode to the far end of town, leaving Ryan to deal with Jenks by himself. Slocum remained in shadow as he watched Kelso ride off. He knew Ryan wouldn't let up until the doctor tended his partner, so he rode slowly after his top hand.

Slocum wasn't sure what he expected to see. If Kelso had tied up with the man out in the valley, that would have been about perfect for Slocum. A quick draw, get the drop on the two men, and then take them to Marshal Zamora to find out what they were up to. The Bar-S had lost close to fifty head of cattle since Wimmer's death. Slocum reckoned a good talking-to with Kelso and any of the men he thought to be rustlers would recover most of the beeves.

Again, Kelso surprised him. The man rode along until he saw a woman dressed in a shimmering white dress hurrying along the boardwalk. Like the needle of a compass, Kelso veered from his course and rode to where he could call out to the woman. Slocum got closer so he could overhear.

"You can't go on denyin' you want me, sweetie," Kelso

called. "Come on. Jist you 'n me. We can find a place real private where nobody could see us—"

"I want nothing to do with you, Mr. Kelso," the woman said angrily. "Leave me alone."

"What'll you do, honey buns? What *kin* you do? If you'd jist say 'yes,' I'd take real good care of you."

She turned so that a ray of light from inside the Prancing Pony shone on her face. Slocum had seen pretty women in Heavenly, but none held a candle to her. Her raven's-wing dark hair glinted with almost blue highlights. Her bow-shaped lips pursed as she worked on what to say to the cowboy. Slocum wasn't able to hear what she did say because it was pitched too low and a considerable ruckus from inside the saloon drowned out her words, but Colorado Pete reared back as if he had been scalded.

"You li'l bitch. Nobody says anythin' like that to me!"

"I did, sir. Leave me alone."

She turned, her white skirt swirling about her ankles. Slocum rode closer, ready to intervene when Kelso jumped to the ground and went to her. His filthy hand left sooty marks on her white sleeve as he spun her around.

She stepped closer and Kelso backed off, hand dropping from her arm when she kneed him in the balls.

"Leave me alone. Can a man with even your small . . . brain understand that?"

"You ain't seen the last of me," Kelso said. He growled like a wild animal, mounted, and galloped away.

Slocum was torn between following Kelso and going to the woman to apologize. She took a deep breath, causing her breasts to rise and fall delightfully under her starched white bodice. This might not have been all that decided him, but it was enough. He dismounted and went to her.

"Ma'am," Slocum said, taking off his hat. "My name's John Slocum, and I saw what happened just now."

"Did you? Is spying on private citizens what you do? And whoever would pay you for such a thing?"

"I . . . work out on the Bar-S Ranch." Slocum saw her stiffen and reach into her purse. The glint of light off a derringer told him what had run off Colorado Pete Kelso—other than being kneed in the groin. She had closed the distance between them and thrust the pistol into Kelso's belly before kicking him. The worst marksman in the world could not have missed at such range with her target being incapacitated.

"It figures," she said.

"No, it doesn't," Slocum said, taking her meaning. Anyone working with Kelso had to be just as boorish. "If he bothers you again, I'll fire him."

"You're foreman at the ranch?"

"I was hired for that very job," Slocum said, not elaborating. If she had been in town, she would have known both his name and that he was the new owner of the Bar-S. For some reason, Slocum thought telling her all that would scare her off. He wanted her to stick around.

"I apologize. It's so seldom I find anyone from the Bar-S with even a speck of civility." She smiled. Just a hint, a small curl of those perfect lips, but her bright blue eyes danced also, telling Slocum she no longer put him in the same box as Colorado Pete Kelso.

"It's me that has to apologize," Slocum said. "Kelso is hardly housebroke, but that's no excuse for bad manners."

"Thanks," she said. "Now, if you'll excuse me, I have to go." She smiled a little more at him and then pushed past. He caught a hint of her perfume. His nostrils flared even as his imagination ran wild. Slocum turned to see her get into a buggy parked in the alley alongside the saloon. She expertly took the reins and snapped them to get her horse moving. With another jerk on the leathers, she headed down the main street in the direction opposite to that taken by Kelso.

He stepped out into the street and watched her disappear into the night. Only when she had gone did he realize he had not asked her name.

"Hey, Mr. Slocum, what're you doin' out in the middle of the street?" Gutherie stepped out from the Prancing Pony. "All the fun's inside. All the whiskey, too."

"Did you see the woman who just passed by?"

"I did," Gutherie said cautiously, as if Slocum intended to trap him into some confession of misdeed.

"Who is she?"

"If you got any sense, you'll give her a wide berth. She's not—well, jist say she's not your type."

"You do know her. What's her name?"

"That's Suzanne Underwood," the barkeep said as if the name burned his tongue.

"She live around town? I haven't seen her before."

"She don't live in town that I know of, and I would if she did. She travels a whole lot. Now, come on in and I'll set you up with a drink. On the house."

Slocum looked sharply at Gutherie. The man was a friendly sort who aimed to please customers. The friendly rivalry, which may not have been all that peaceable at times, with the other saloon counted some toward the offer, but Slocum thought the bar owner only wanted to keep him away from Suzanne Underwood.

"I've got other business to tend to. Thanks."

"Make that a rain check. You come in any time tonight 'fore midnight, you get the free shot of whiskey."

Slocum nodded. Gutherie looked almost fearfully in the direction Suzanne Underwood had driven, and hurried back into the saloon. Slocum stared into the distance, wondering where Kelso had got himself off to—and wondering about Suzanne Underwood. He finally shook his head. Small towns developed likes and hates as if they were people. Whatever Suzanne Underwood had done—or not done—had made at least one of the townsfolk scared to even talk about her.

"A man could get into a powerful lot of trouble with a woman who looks like her," Slocum said to himself. He wondered how much trouble he was willing to get into.

Slocum mounted and swung his horse around to ride past the doctor's surgery. Gainsborough's wife, Nora, stood outside. She smiled at him as he rode up.

"Coming to check on your cowhand?"

"Reckon I am. How's he doing?"

"Ben got the cut all stitched up. Didn't look too fearsome, but you know how head wounds tend to bleed. You got him to help in time."

"Glad to hear that. Would you tell Ryan to stay with Jenks, if that's all right with Doc Gainsborough?"

"Ryan didn't say anything about you coming to town. He said he left you out in the high meadow running down rustlers."

"Got tired of that," Slocum said. "Or maybe not." From the corner of his eye, he saw Kelso riding past in a mighty big hurry. "Much obliged for looking after Jenks." Slocum touched the brim of his hat and tore out after Kelso.

The man rode so hard that Slocum lost him within a half mile of town. Rather than keep chasing him and maybe lose him in the dark, Slocum veered off the road and went to higher ground. He might spot a dust cloud and get some idea what had gotten Kelso so fired up.

It took the better part of an hour to make his way through the rocks and onto a ridge looking out over the road leading from Heavenly into a small valley on the other side. The almost full moon had risen, giving the land a silver aspect that made it about the most beautiful thing Slocum had ever seen. A coyote howled in the distance, but the animals moving close by betrayed the abundant life in the area. There was the slither of a snake and the thump of a rabbit running, the heavier tread of a fox and maybe even the soft snarl of a mountain lion. It was all there, mingled with the smells of things growing and cattle grazing.

Slocum traced out the main road the best he could in the dark, but Kelso was nowhere to be seen. He turned his attention to the valley, wondering who grazed their cattle here.

A small herd, hardly twenty head, moved fitfully in the night. They might be searching for water, or there might be some other reason to get them moving.

Slocum worked his way down the slope. The mountain lion might be hunting for a late-night dinner—or there might be two-legged predators on the prowl. If the rustlers couldn't make off with Bar-S cattle whenever they wanted anymore, they might move on to other spreads.

It didn't matter to Slocum whose land he rode on if he bagged a rustler or two.

He made his way down the slope opposite to town, finding this less rocky. By the time he reached the bottom of the ridge, he had found a narrow, winding road. He turned in the saddle, spotted the Big Dipper with its pointer stars, and finally located the North Star to orient himself. With the moonlight so bright it was almost like riding on a cloudy day, he turned to ride deeper into the valley. Then he heard a horse coming from behind, probably from town. He had never noticed the turnoff from the main road onto this one because there had been no reason to come this way before.

Might be that Colorado Pete Kelso had found some reason, since Slocum couldn't figure anyone else who might be out riding at this time of night. He trotted off the road to a shallow arroyo where he could watch for the approaching rider. Less than five minutes passed before he saw a solitary horseman. The man had his hat pulled down and was all hunched over, and Slocum couldn't identify him. It might have been Kelso, but it as easily could have been President Grant out for a midnight ride.

The rider suddenly halted and looked around, seemingly staring straight at Slocum. Wheeling about suddenly, the rider rocketed away. Slocum considered the matter for a moment, then his curiosity got the better of him. If this was Kelso, he wanted to ask his top hand what he was doing here. If it was a rustler, Slocum could eliminate one more of the bastards. And what man out for honest reasons would hightail it like that?

Putting his heels to his roan's flanks, Slocum got out of the arroyo and onto the narrow road. It was not as smooth as the main road because it didn't have as much traffic, but Slocum could rely on the bright moonlight to avoid any prairie-dog holes or potholes that might cause his horse any trouble.

He urged his horse to a faster gait, watching the road for trouble.

He should have watched alongside the road for snipers. The shot tore past his face so close he felt the bullet's hot breath against his cheek. Involuntarily, he reached up and touched the heated spot, expecting his hand to come away bloody. The bullet had not even broken skin.

Slocum pulled back hard on the reins and got his horse to stop. He studied the terrain for a likely spot for the sniper to hide. He saw nothing, but heard pounding hoofbeats going away. Rather than pursue blindly, Slocum rode ahead a few yards, wary of a trap. He had seen one rider. If the man was a rustler, he might have several cronies with him. All of them could be lying in wait.

The thunder of the hooves faded in the distance, and Slocum heard nothing else but the soft wind blowing across the valley. He inhaled deeply. Grass. Cattle. Good earth. The scent of things alive and flourishing. But it carried no scent of men.

Slocum touched his cheek again and winced. The slug had not broken the skin, but it felt as if it had burned a path. He snapped the reins and brought the roan to a gallop. Bending low, Slocum intended to present the smallest target possible if he did ride into another trap.

But after another mile down the road, he had not been on the receiving end of any more gunfire. He thought the rider he had spotted was also the unseen sniper. Not only did the man want to keep his identity a secret, he was willing to kill, too.

As his horse began to tire, Slocum slowed. As he came to

a trot, he caught a flash of silver out of the corner of his eye. Slocum bent lower and slowed his horse more, swinging it around in a wide circle. He approached the spot from the far side. Shadows and the confusion of shapes made it difficult to tell what he had seen. Slocum jumped to the ground and drew his six-shooter as he approached.

A buggy wheel turned slowly, spun by the rising wind. When he realized this was what had caught his attention, he walked faster. Details fell into place. A buggy had overturned on the road and rolled over completely at least once to end up on its side. The contents of the buggy littered the slope all the way to the road.

Of the buggy's horse, he saw nothing.

But as to its driver, he saw her pinned under the broken driver's seat.

Slocum knelt beside Suzanne Underwood and pressed his hand against her throat. Her pulse was thready and her breathing shallow.

She was alive.

9

Slocum got a grip on the edge of the buggy and lifted it away from the unconscious woman. Suzanne Underwood moaned enough to let him know she wasn't close to dead yet. He worried that a broken piece of wood from the side of the buggy might have impaled her. Getting his feet squarely under him, he heaved and threw the buggy onto its wheels. It tottered for a moment, and then ran on downhill a few more feet before stopping. The back wheel slanted at a crazy angle and the seat was entirely out of kilter.

Kneeling again, Slocum cradled her head. The woman's dark hair carried streaks of dried blood. He smoothed those away from her face. In the moonlight, she seemed more dead than alive, but her lips, appearing black, moved as she muttered something. He bent over and listened, but could not understand what she said.

"Come on," Slocum said, getting his arms around her so he could lift her from the ground. He staggered a little on the slope and went to his horse. The roan smelled the fresh blood and shied away, forcing Slocum to put Suzanne down and catch at the reins so he could drag the horse back toward him. He unlooped his canteen from the saddle and dripped water on her lips. They looked deathly black in the moonlight, but he knew that any red turned this shade. He had seen more than his share of blood this color at night.

"Umm, what . . ." She tried to sit up, but he gently held her down.

"You rolled your buggy over. Lie still. You've got quite a bump on the side of your head."

Slocum watched her reaction closely. Some men with as hard a blow as Suzanne had sustained never woke up. She was lucky.

"You're from town. Mr. Slocum?" Again, she tried to sit up. He pushed her back down. "Oh, posh, let me go. I'm not a one to be coddled."

Slocum rocked back and let her struggle to her feet. She was shaky, but managed to take a few steps without falling over.

"What happened?"

"I . . . that's not too clear." Suzanne touched the side of her head and winced. Even this light touch reopened her wound. "I was driving along and hit a rock. The wheel wobbled. I remember that. The buggy veered, my horse began bucking, and the next thing I remember clearly is seeing you." She smiled wanly. "Thank you."

"I might be able to fix your buggy and get you on your way."

"My horse ran off."

"Horses don't run too far, even scared ones. If the buggy will roll along without the wheels falling off, finding the horse will be easy enough." Slocum cocked his head to one side and judged that sunrise was only an hour or so away. Finding her horse wouldn't be too difficult then. He hadn't passed the horse, so it must have either run back in the direction Suzanne had come from, or taken off to one side of the road or the other.

They went back to her buggy. Slocum grabbed her around the waist as she stumbled.

"Thank you again, Mr. Slocum. I don't seem as steady on my feet as I had thought."

"That was quite a bump you got," Slocum said. He saw the swollen lump oozing blood through the tangle of her dark hair. "We need to find a stream and get it washed off."

"My buggy first," she said. In spite of her insistence on this, she didn't pull away from Slocum, so he kept his arm around her. She made a tidy bundle, her hip bumping against his as they looked at the buggy's damage.

"I can get that wheel nut tightened," he said, shaking the right wheel. "I don't have the tools, but any rancher would have them. Where were you heading?"

"Seamus Murphy's ranch is the closest," she said.

Slocum wondered why she was going there, then realized she had not said she was—not exactly. Her knowledge of the countryside was better than his, although he had been in Middle Park for some time now. The times he had ridden across Murphy's ranch he had been chasing after rustlers.

"Might be just as good to go back to Heavenly and get the tools there," he said.

"I can wait for you," she said, but her tone implied that wasn't what she wanted to do. She looked around, just a touch of consternation on her lovely face.

Slocum had his own problem with her remaining alone. The rustler who had taken a potshot at him was still roaming around, possibly with several others of his gang. Leaving Suzanne Underwood alone was a foolish thing to do in her condition.

"I can look for your horse, but it might be for the best if you'd just ride behind. I can get the tools, fix your buggy, and track down your horse while you rest up in town."

"That's not the sort of place for me to rest. Not after—"

"After what?"

"You're about the only one in town who'll even speak to me, Mr. Slocum."

"Why are they bound and determined to treat you like an outcast?"

"I'd rather not burden you with my tale of woe, sir," she said.

From the set to her shoulders and the way her lips thinned to little more than a razor slash, he knew prying the information from her would be difficult. Although curious, Slocum didn't care that much about small-town gossip and small-minded gossips.

He swung into the saddle and reached down so she could take his hand. With a smooth motion, he pulled her up behind him. She settled down and put her arms around his waist. It made being shot at worthwhile.

"Next stop, Heavenly, Colorado," he said. His roan tiredly plodded away. Slocum decided he was in no particular hurry since he enjoyed the feel of Suzanne so close behind him. She laid her cheek against his back as they rode. He felt her even breathing, and wondered if she had fallen asleep after a couple miles.

Slocum fell into the easy rhythm of the horse, warmed by Suzanne's arms around him and her body pressing tightly against his. The shot that sang through the still, early morning took him completely by surprise.

"Hang on," he called to Suzanne. She lurched and almost tumbled from horseback as he bent forward and put his spurs to his horse's flanks. Barely had the horse run a dozen yards when another shot rang out.

Slocum went sailing through the air, Suzanne still clinging to him. His horse's front legs crumpled and its head hit the ground. After that, Slocum was not sure what happened. He skidded along the road on his belly with Suzanne clinging to him. By the time he came to a halt, Slocum was torn up and bloody and madder than hell.

He stood and the dark-haired woman slid to one side, sitting in the dirt and staring numbly at him.

"Stay down," he snarled. Slocum slapped leather. His Colt

Navy came easily to his hand, but he could not find a target. He slowly turned to his left, hunting for the spot where the sniper had fired. Nothing moved in the dim light of predawn. Knowing it was foolish, Slocum fired several times at clumps of vegetation likely to hide a rifleman. Dust and dried leaves were kicked up, but nobody was flushed from hiding.

Knowing better than to continue firing wildly, Slocum reached down and grabbed Suzanne's hand. He dragged her upright.

"Go," he said. "Run. I'll cover you."

"Who's shooting at us?"

"Go!"

A foot-long tongue of orange flame licked out from a spot not fifty yards away. The distance was too great for a handgun, but Slocum emptied his six-gun and succeeded in driving the sniper back under cover. He backed away, then untied his saddlebags and slung them over his shoulder. His spare ammo was inside, as well as a spare pistol. Only when he had reloaded did he go after Suzanne. The woman had run farther than he expected. She was either more scared than he had anticipated, or she had taken his warning to heart.

"Go higher," he ordered. "Into the rocks. We can get under cover there."

"I . . . I'm out of breath." He heard a rasp that sounded as bad as if she had tuberculosis.

"You'll be out of breath forever if you don't keep going." Slocum swung about and damned himself for not bringing his Winchester along, too. He aimed at the bushes where the sniper had been, adjusted for the fitful wind, and elevated his muzzle to arc his round into the vegetation. His first shot missed by yards. His second took off a twig at the side of the bushes. A third shot hit dead center. Slocum stopped firing and waited.

This time he was met with a volley of rifle fire from three different positions. The men were all bad marksmen, but they threw enough lead in his direction to force him back, again cursing that he had left his rifle behind.

"John, are you all right?"

"Keep moving. Go higher. Into the hills. There are at least three of them after us."

"Three?" Suzanne said weakly. "Who are they?"

"Probably rustlers," he said. "It doesn't much matter who they are. All I need to know is that they shot my horse, and if we don't keep moving, they'll shoot the both of us."

Slocum hung back as Suzanne made her way through the rocks. Tracking her progress was easy because of her labored breathing. He shifted position, expecting the rustlers to come after them. The more he thought, the more he reckoned that these were some of the varmints still remaining on the range to steal his beeves. Not only his, since they were on the wrong side of the mountains, but Seamus Murphy's also.

He waited close to ten minutes, letting the first blush of sunrise scrape across the eastern sky. He peered into the rising sun and then went after Suzanne. He did what he could to cover their tracks. She had left a trail a blind man could follow. After a half hour, he stopped and stared at a sheer, stony face with three caves in it.

He looked for tracks, but she had left none across the rocky ground. Unerringly, he went to the cave on the right.

"Suzanne, how deep's the cave?"

"How'd you know which I picked? There are three."

"This was the only one with a bear in it," he said.

She let out a yelp and rushed out. He caught her in his arms and spun her around. Her feet fought for traction, but he held her off the ground.

"Bears! I didn't know. We can't—" She looked into his green eyes and got mad then.

She hit him with her fist as she said, "You're joshing me!"

"Was a bit of fun, I admit," he said, putting her back onto the floor of the cave.

"You scared me."

"There's no bear in here," Slocum said.

"How'd you know I'd pick this one? I didn't even look at the other two."

"Folks tend to bend to the right when they choose. Get lost in the desert and you'll walk in circles, always heading to the right and never knowing it."

"I didn't know that," she said, "but then I've never been lost in the desert. I prefer land with more contours." Suzanne sat down on a rock and looked up at him. "Are they going to find us? The men who shot at us?"

"I waited to see. They might have decided killing my horse was good enough for the night. If they are rustlers, they're probably not too inclined to face a man when they shoot at him. Too much chance he'll shoot back. I made it clear that I wasn't going to let them simply murder me."

Her bright blue eyes drifted to the six-gun in its cross-draw holster.

"You have the look of a man who's accustomed to using his six-shooter."

Slocum dropped his saddlebags and then sat on the floor of the cave opposite Suzanne. He paused a moment before saying anything. It had been fun getting his arms around her, just as hers had been around him during their short ride. She was a mighty fine-looking woman, even with her black hair all mussed and dirt smudges on her face. The way she sat, her skirt was hiked up so he could see her ankles and even some of her bare legs.

She noticed his attention, and pulled her skirt up a mite farther, giving him a flash of her inner thigh.

"You think they'll be here any time soon?" She pulled her skirt up even more. "So we would have enough time?"

"Enough time for what?" Slocum felt himself getting harder, thinking about how he would while away an hour or so.

"For me to thank you. You saved my life."

"Maybe not. You took quite a bump on the head, but—" Slocum didn't get any further. Suzanne rose, gathered her skirts, and stepped forward, putting her feet on either side of his legs. She lowered herself slowly, swishing the skirt about seductively. Her butt settled down on his upper thighs.

Their faces were only inches apart. Slocum reached up, laced his fingers through her tangled hair, and pulled her face to his for a satisfying kiss. Their passion built until they were devouring each other. When her red lips parted just a little, Slocum's tongue worked its way into her mouth for a bit of erotic dueling. She was moaning softly now, and her breasts heaved under her bodice. Without breaking off the kiss, Slocum slipped his hand from the back of her head and pressed it into her breasts. Even through the thick cloth he felt her nipple hardening. He squeezed down until she sobbed aloud with need.

"Oh, John, John," she whispered hotly. "I want you so."

She rearranged her skirt and reached down to find the buttons on his fly. By now he was achingly hard. His erection finally popped up long and proud when she pulled open the last of his buttons. They both gasped when she rose slightly, positioned herself, and then lowered her hips. His erection slid into her hot, slick core.

She cried out at the intrusion. Slocum fought to keep from getting off like some young buck with his first woman. She was tight around him, and when she moved about, it pulled and squeezed at him in delightfully new ways.

She began moving, rising, twisting about, lowering herself in a back-and-forth swish of her hips. Every time she took him fully, she tensed around him, paused for deliciously long moments, and only then did she begin to rise. He slid in and out with increasing friction that burned and boiled.

He pushed away her bodice and exposed a breast. He took it firmly into his mouth—as much as he could cram in. The marshmallowy flesh yielded slightly as he pressed his tongue into the hard nub until it pushed back. Then he caught only the coppery nip between his lips and sucked powerfully as she continued to rise and fall around his hardness.

They each gave as good as they got. Suzanne sped up. Slocum stroked over her back and cupped her buttocks. His mouth explored her breasts and the deep canyon between them. And then they could not restrain themselves a moment longer. She might have got off before he did. Slocum couldn't be sure—and it hardly mattered. Locked together, they struggled to share even more of one another, and then Suzanne sank down on his lap, her head resting on his shoulder. Her hot, ragged breath came in his ear as she whispered, "You went limp on me."

"Wasn't for lack of trying to keep it up longer."

She laughed and sat back. Her eyes danced.

"It's *my* turn to josh you. That was wonderful, John. I need you saving my life more often so I can reward you again."

"Don't need one to get the other," he said. She laughed at this and got off his lap, sitting beside him in the cave. Their arms pressed together; then Suzanne lifted her leg and draped it on top of his before laying her head on his shoulder.

"I wish we could just stay here like this forever."

"Forever's a long time," he said.

"You really own the Bar-S?"

The question took him by surprise. All he had told her was that he worked there as foreman.

"Reckon so. Don't know what made Wimmer give it to me, but he did. I've never owned a spread that large or profitable."

"The son of a bitch," she said. Acid dripped from every word as she gripped his arm hard. Her fingers dug into his flesh until he wondered how badly he would be bruised.

"You didn't cotton much to Jackson Wimmer? Doesn't seem that many in Heavenly did. I'd think you and the townsfolk would have that in common."

"I hated the ground he walked on."

"I'm the one walking on it now," Slocum said. Her death grip on his arm lessened. "What did you have against Wimmer?"

"How'd he die?"

"There's some debate going on about that. Colorado Pete Kelso found a six-shooter beside the body but that gun wasn't Wimmer's. That makes it look to be murder."

"Murder? I'm not surprised."

"Kelso and, I reckon, Marshal Zamora think it was a rancher out this way named Seamus Murphy who did it."

"No!"

Slocum considered her angry denial.

"He didn't do it," he finally said. "He was getting drunk with me in the Prancing Pony about the time Wimmer got himself shot."

"Are you and Mr. Murphy drinking buddies?"

"I wouldn't call it that. He has a powerful lot of anger dammed up inside for anyone to be his friend." Slocum considered how alike Seamus and Suzanne were in this regard. The mere mention of Jackson Wimmer set her off.

"Who do you think killed him?" she asked.

"I can't say, but I have my suspicions."

"Kelso," she said firmly. "It was Kelso. He's as much a bastard as Wimmer. Well, not that much. He's got a mean streak, too, but he's not evil down deep where it counts."

"You seem to have them pegged pretty well. What did you have against Wimmer?"

Slocum couldn't ask any more directly than that, and again Suzanne Underwood edged away from directly answering. She slipped down so she lay on the cave floor, her face in his lap. Slocum wasn't about to press for an answer when her lips were put to a better use than answering foolish questions.

10

"Are you still dizzy?" Slocum asked. He watched as Suzanne Underwood tried to stand. She had to brace herself against the cave wall, and even then her legs proved wobbly.

"I don't know what it can be. I was fine last night."

"You were more than fine," he assured her. They had remained in the cave throughout the previous day, waiting to see if any of the rustlers tracked them down. Slocum had watched from a vantage point higher up on the mountainside and had seen no one in the peaceful valley where they had been ambushed. Even so, he had decided it was better to lie low and let Suzanne rest. The bump on her head refused to stop oozing blood, no matter what he did to stanch the flow. He had seen wounds like that before, and they usually took care of themselves with rest. Having to hike back to Heavenly was not going to help her in the least.

In spite of his determination to have her do nothing but rest during the night, their activities together had been anything but restful. In a way, he was glad he didn't have to mount up and ride off right now since he was a mite sore. Clambering over the rocks proved strain enough.

"Thank you, John. You—oh!"

He caught her as she slipped and fell. She would have

landed facedown if he had not swung her around and eased her to the cave floor.

"You're going to have to rest up. I'll go on into town and get the tools I need to fix your buggy."

"That's a long walk."

He considered this, and remembered all he had seen while he had been atop the butte looking into Murphy's pastureland. Another way might exist that wouldn't require him to leave her for as long as a trip into Heavenly would take.

"It's closer for me to keep going over this mountain and get onto Bar-S land. If I'm lucky, I can find one of my cowboys and ride with him to the ranch house." The words rang true but odd to his ears. He was the owner of a vast ranch. He was more used to being the one riding the range for someone else.

"That sounds better. I'm not sure anyone in town would give you the time of day if you told them what you wanted the tools for."

"You don't like those people much, do you?"

"It's mutual."

Slocum almost asked why again, and then held his tongue. Even being straightforward with his questions about Jackson Wimmer and how Suzanne lived and why she didn't get along with the townspeople produced no answers. She flat out would not answer, and he saw no reason to pursue it now.

"I don't like leaving you, but I don't have much choice. Can you use a six-gun?"

"I can." Suzanne did not hesitate with her answer. Slocum took that to mean she was being truthful. He rummaged about in his saddlebags and found his spare Colt Navy. It took a few minutes for him to check its action and to load it before handing it to her. She expertly checked the chambers again, then lowered the hammer slowly.

"It's a good idea you have, letting the hammer rest on an empty chamber," she said. He nodded in agreement. She had done more than pretend to make certain the six-gun was in good condition. She had actually examined it and understood what she was doing.

With a quick kiss, he left her. The sun poked above the eastern horizon again, today promising rain. Leaden gray clouds floated in the distance, coming off the Rockies and swooping westward toward them like misty soldiers to a battle. For the moment there wasn't much to worry about, but as the day warmed, the rain would begin pelting down.

Slocum hitched up his gun belt and began the hike. He kept his bearing as true as he could when he topped the ridge and worked down on the far side. By noon he recognized the sprawl of a meadow—his meadow.

He took a deep whiff and caught the odor of wood smoke and coffee. Homing in on it like a hawk to a rabbit, he found two of his hands enjoying a midday meal.

"Howdy, men," he said, flopping down across from them. "You got a cup of coffee for the boss?"

"Yes, sir, Mr. Slocum. Didn't hear you ride up."

Slocum took the proffered tin cup filled to the brim with barely drinkable coffee. It was too hot and too bitter and tasted as good as anything he had ever drunk. After he finished, he told them what had happened.

"You want us to git on over the hill and chase them varmints down?"

"No, I need to get back to the ranch house and scare up some tools to fix Miss Underwood's buggy," he said. One of the men frowned. The other looked more concerned with the rustlers. Slocum had to ask the one who frowned, "You been in Middle Park long?"

"Came to Heavenly more than a year back."

"So you know what the trouble is between Miss Underwood and the people in town." The words were hardly out of his mouth when he realized the cowboy wasn't going to tell him anything either. For such a friendly small town, the residents clammed up when it came to what ought to be gossip shared freely.

Slocum rode double with one of the hands, and got back to the ranch by mid-afternoon. He looked around for Kelso, but did not see him. Rather than ask, Slocum found a horse to replace his roan, again marveling that all the horses in the corral behind the barn were his, then threw tools into a buckboard and hitched up a double team. He remembered to fetch a rifle and ammo from the house before leaving.

The hands loitering around the ranch watched him leave. Some whispered among themselves, having heard his story from the two men he had ridden back with, but the others stared at him with something approaching anger. Slocum knew that Colorado Pete had been sowing the seeds of discontent, inciting them to anger over not having the ranch put up for sale and the proceeds divvied up among the lot of them.

He made good time down the main road and along the spur running off it. This portion of the trip was enough to knock his teeth out. Rocks and potholes in the narrow road forced him to drive slower than he liked, but he soon got to where Suzanne's buggy had taken a tumble down the verge of the road. He jumped down, gathered his tools, and worked for twenty minutes straightening the wheel by tightening the nut holding it. He unhitched one horse from his team and put it to the buggy, and got back to the road without having to exert himself any more than necessary.

Slocum wiped sweat from his face as he studied the mountain where he and Suzanne had taken refuge. He tied the horse pulling the buggy onto the rear of the buckboard on the far side from his new horse, a gelding that stepped along with an assured gait. He preferred the roan, now dead some distance back along the road, but the gelding would serve him well.

Driving with one eye on the grassy expanse around him, he reached a spot at the foothills. He heaved a sigh. It was a long climb up and if Suzanne had passed out, it would be an even longer trip back down. He wrapped the reins around the brake and started to get down when he heard the click of pebbles tumbling down the slope. Without seeming too obvious, he grabbed the rifle and kept turning, dropping to the ground. As he turned, he cocked the rifle and brought it to his shoulder. He sighted in on Suzanne Underwood slipping and sliding down the slope.

"You made good time," she said. She struggled with the canteen and his saddlebags. "Want to help me? You must carry gold bricks in here." With a heave, she got the saddlebags off her shoulder. He saw how she was still shaky on her feet.

"I would have fetched you."

"You make it sound like I'm a bone to be retrieved by some hungry dog," she said tartly. Another step and she sagged. He caught her and got her into the back of the buckboard.

"I need to get my gear, then we can head for town."

Suzanne didn't answer. She had drifted off. He made her as comfortable as he could, turned around, and drove to where his dead horse lay gathering flies. It took the better part of twenty minutes to pull his gear off the dead horse. He was less interested in the saddle and rifle as he was the saddle blanket. The saddle provided a pillow for Suzanne and the blanket cushioned some of the shock driving over the rocky road. He finally reached the road into Heavenly, and drove in just past sundown. Even so, people came out and watched. It was as if he had a sign saying he and Suzanne Underwood were riding together.

They might not see her, but they recognized her buggy. Slocum drove straight for Doc Gainsborough's office. He was relieved to see a light still burning in the window. A knock on the door was answered promptly. The doctor looked tired, but a faint grin crept to his lips when he recognized Slocum.

"You bringin' me more patients? I declare, Slocum, since you took over the Bar-S, my business has about doubled."

"In the back of the buckboard," Slocum said. Ben Gainsborough went out with him. When he saw his patient, he looked sharply at Slocum.

"She agree to letting me tend her?"

"She's not in much condition to agree to anything. She took a whack to the side of the head." Slocum related how her buggy wheel had come loose and sent her tumbling down the side of the road into an arroyo.

"That's not her horse."

"Mine. I had to hike back to the Bar-S for the buckboard and horses after my horse got shot out from under me."

Gainsborough waited as Slocum related even more of the story. All Slocum held back was how he and Suzanne had spent the previous day and the previous night in the cave.

"You might consider opening an account with me," Gainsborough said. "You're trying to triple my business, not that such a thing would be hard, considering."

Slocum looked curiously at the doctor, wondering what he meant. There wasn't another doctor between here and Montrose. Ben Gainsborough must tend about everyone in town. Before he could ask, the doctor gestured impatiently for Slocum to help him.

Together, they wrestled a limp Suzanne from the buckboard and into the surgery. As they laid her on the examination table, Nora Gainsborough came in.

"Oh, no, what happened?"

"You can tell her, Doc," Slocum said. "I'm going to get some medicine of my own."

"Knock back a shot or two of Gutherie's medicine for me, too," Gainsborough said. As Slocum left, he saw the doctor take his wife by the arm and steer her to the corner of the room, where they exchanged words in a whisper. Nora Gainsborough forced her way past her husband, and went to the table and placed her hand on Suzanne's forehead. Slocum closed the door and stepped into the cool Colorado night. It had been a hell of a couple days and he didn't have much to show for it.

Other than a delightful day and night spent in a cave with about the most beautiful woman in this part of Colorado.

"And the most mysterious," he said to himself as he went into the Prancing Pony.

"Hey, Mr. Slocum, you're too late fer that free drink," Gutherie told him.

"That's all right. I'm willing to pay for a shot or two."

"Or more?" Gutherie winked at him. Slocum nodded. He took a half bottle, went to a table at the side of the saloon, and sank down. The chair creaked almost as much as his joints. He wasn't used to walking so far, and he was even still a tad sore from his and Suzanne's lovemaking.

As he worked on his second shot, the saloon doors opened and swung shut behind a short man with a nose that twitched and a wispy mustache that made him look like a San Francisco wharf rat. He surveyed the room, then came straight for Slocum.

"I got a proposition fer you, Mr. Slocum."

"You've got the advantage on me. You know my name. Who're you?"

"Robertson, Rupert Robertson, but my friends call me Roop."

"You have many friends, Rupert?" Slocum saw how the question that should have irritated most men only sailed past him. Roop Robertson was intent on something more than conversation as he sank down into the chair opposite Slocum. He leaned forward, elbows on the table. Slocum was no spring daisy after all he had been through, but the smell from Robertson's lack of bathing almost gagged him.

"You're the new owner of the Bar-S." The way he said it didn't require any response from Slocum. Robertson hurried on, as if trying to say everything before he forgot it. "I want to buy the Bar-S. I'll pay a fair price fer it."

"Do tell."

"We kin git the town clerk to draw up the papers and—"

"I don't want to sell."

Robertson blinked as if the dim light from the coal oil lamps around the room was too intense for his weak eyes.

"But I'm willin' to *pay* fer it. You didn't even hear my offer."

"Doesn't matter. The Bar-S isn't for sale."

"I'll make it worth yer while. Real money. Cash money."

"No." Slocum saw Robertson's shocked reaction. The man started to argue and Slocum again said, "No." This time he drew his six-gun and laid it on the table to punctuate his answer.

"You'll regret it. Mark my words, you'll damn well regret it."

Robertson shot to his feet and stormed out of the saloon. Slocum watched the doors swing, then slowly poured himself another drink. Life was certainly different being the owner of a big ranch.

Slocum reached for his pistol when the doors opened again. He relaxed when he saw Doc Gainsborough come in. The man made a beeline for him and sat in the chair Robertson had just vacated.

"A drink?" Slocum pushed the bottle in the doctor's direction.

With a curt shake of his head, Gainsborough declined. He put his forearms on the table and leaned forward so no one could overhear. Somehow, Slocum didn't mind the old doctor doing this. When Robertson had tried to be all private with him, he had wanted to punch the man's ratlike face.

"She's going to be all right," Gainsborough said without preamble, "but you've got to get her out of town."

"Folks don't take much to her, do they? Neither does your wife."

This shocked Gainsborough. He straightened and started to say something, but no words came out. Slocum wondered at the shock.

He wondered even more when Gainsborough asked, "Are you selling the Bar-S?"

"Seems to be a subject that's getting a whole lot more discussion than it's worth," Slocum said. "A fellow just offered to buy it. I turned him down. Are you wanting to buy it, too?"

"No, of course not," Gainsborough said, his hand flying through the air in a dismissive motion. "In fact, I hope you don't sell it. You really ought to—"

"Hold on to your thought," Slocum said. "Looks like the marshal's joining us." Louder, Slocum said, "Evening, Marshal. You want a snort?" He held up the whiskey bottle. Zamora's eyes fixed on the bottle and he licked his lips, then shook his head about the same way Gainsborough already had.

"Heard you were back in town, Slocum," Marshal Zamora said. He hooked his thumbs in his gun belt and hitched it up under his bulging belly. "Also heard you were out at Murphy's place. What'd the two of you talk about?"

"Never saw him, Marshal. Got shot at, probably by rustlers I haven't run off yet."

"He did it, Slocum. I want you to be on guard. Seamus Murphy killed Wimmer."

"Just because his gun was found by the body?" Slocum had no desire to go over his alibi for the young rancher since Zamora had already heard it and obviously dismissed it.

"The two of them had a blood feud going. Never saw two men hate like they did. It was murder, pure and simple, and Murphy did it."

"Can't help you prove that, Marshal," said Slocum. "In court, I'd have to testify against your theory."

"Might be you and him are in cahoots. You knew the will had been changed so you get him to murder Wimmer. You and him gonna divvy up the spoils?"

Slocum sighed and then said, "The barkeep can testify we were both in the Prancing Pony about the time Wimmer died."

"Bennett's nowhere to be seen. Might be he didn't run off with Lulu like everyone thinks. Might be you or Murphy killed him since he could say you and Murphy wasn't drinking together in the bar."

Slocum closed his eyes, took a deep breath, and then stared straight at the marshal. Arguing with a man whose mind was as set as Zamora's was wearing him down. He tried a different argument.

"I didn't know the will had been changed. Wimmer never told me. And if there was such bad blood between the two of them, Murphy would have been the last to know that Wimmer had changed his will."

"You're right. Maybe he just shot Wimmer out of spite."

"You have any other suspects?" Slocum watched the marshal carefully and read the answer before the lawman spoke.

"Don't need no one else. Even if I believe what you say, Murphy did the deed. All I need to do is prove it. He's as clever as he is mean."

"Mighty careless of a man doing so much planning to leave behind the murder weapon," Slocum said.

"Panicked. It's not as easy to kill a man as it seems."

"No, it's not," Slocum agreed. This rocked Zamora back. Their eyes met, and the marshal finally broke off.

"Don't go leaving town, Slocum, not till the trial."

"Are you arresting Murphy?"

"I'm gatherin' the evidence now. Don't have it all yet, but I will."

"I'll be at the ranch," Slocum said. "I don't intend to sell out any time soon."

All this garnered from the marshal was a scowl. He hitched up his belt again and left.

"It has been quite a day," Slocum said, pouring another shot and knocking it back. He had downed another and was beginning to feel the effect now. Accumulated aches and pains faded into distant memory and comforting warmth crept through his body and brain.

"I don't think Murphy killed him either," Gainsborough

said unexpectedly. "There wasn't any call for that because he was dying anyhow."

"Come again?" Slocum tried to push the buzz in his ears away. His thirst had gotten the better of him and now he was hearing things.

"If you can leave the bottle for a few minutes, come on over to the undertaker. I want to show you what I mean."

Slocum got to his feet and trailed Doc Gainsborough from the saloon after shouting at Gutherie not to touch the remainder of the bottle. He and Gainsborough walked in silence to the undertaker's parlor. The doctor went around to the side, rapped twice, and then went in. Slocum followed. The smell of embalming fluids made him a tad dizzy.

"Evening, Lowell. I want Slocum to see what you got from poor old Jackson's gut." Gainsborough went to a shelf and took down a jar with a blackened, withered blob in it.

"You want that, Ben? Ain't no way I want to keep it here. If anybody saw it, it'd be plenty bad for business."

"That's an undertaker for you," Gainsborough said, holding up the jar with its ugly burden. "Doesn't mind dead folks, but things he takes out of them make him squeamish." He handed the jar to Slocum.

"What is it?"

"What's left of Jackson Wimmer's belly."

"Was Wimmer your patient?" Slocum asked the doctor.

"Jackson? No, he was too stubborn for that. Refused to see me or any doctor. But I suspected what Lowell here found out when he was digging around inside, getting him ready to be worm food. Cancer. Wimmer was dying of stomach cancer."

"That would have killed him for certain sure," Lowell said, tapping the side of the jar and stirring the tumor within.

"How long would he have lived if he hadn't caught a bullet in the head?" Slocum asked.

Gainsborough and Lowell exchanged looks. Finally, the doctor said, "Months at the outside. Probably only a couple weeks. Whoever killed him did Jackson Wimmer a favor."

Slocum stared at the jar with the remains of Wimmer's stomach, then put it back on the shelf. In spite of what the undertaker said, he thought the man was going to keep the tumor-riddled stomach as a souvenir. All Slocum wanted to do was return to the saloon and finish his bottle of whiskey. It had been one hell of a couple days.

11

Slocum perched on the top rail of the corral, watching the horses mill about. He had come here to pick another horse. The gelding lacked the stamina Slocum needed for protracted riding out on the range. He had chased two men he thought were rustlers, only to have the gelding tire quickly. Slocum had lost the men.

While they might have been riders on their way south and just happened to cross his property, he wasn't so sure.

"Damn me, I'm jumping at shadows," Slocum said to the horses in the corral. They shied away and gathered in a tight knot of horseflesh at the far side. Although all were saddle broke, the horses chose to reject human contact and preferred the company of others of their kind. Slocum understood how they felt.

He stared at the horses, but hardly noticed them since his thoughts were flying far beyond the corral. Suzanne had been patched up and had left Heavenly the next day, according to what Doc Gainsborough said. Slocum had wanted to see her before she disappeared, but that wasn't in the cards. Neither the doctor nor his wife knew where Suzanne was heading. Considering the scarcity of towns in this part of Colorado, he doubted she had gone too far and figured she would be back eventually. In spite of traveling in her buggy, she lived like a gypsy, always on the move and never lighting for long. He didn't understand her or why the people in Heavenly acted the way they did toward her. In spite of this mystery, Slocum had other things on his mind.

What worried at him like a dog with a bone was selling the Bar-S. It was lagniappe that came from a totally unexpected source. Jackson Wimmer had been an old cuss and, from all that the townspeople said, one who delighted in causing a ruckus. Giving Slocum the entire ranch had done that as surely as a royal flush swept the pot every time. Colorado Pete Kelso wanted Slocum to sell. That disreputable rat-faced man, Rupert Robertson, wanted to buy. The only problem lay in Slocum not knowing what he wanted to do about the ranch.

The Bar-S was profitable, and getting the herd to the railhead and market in a few weeks would put a considerable roll of greenbacks in his pocket. But selling meant he would move on, always chasing after the clouds on the horizon, hunting for that which had no name. Slocum was satisfied enough doing that. After so many years, it suited him. But if he settled down, it could be with a woman like Suzanne Underwood. It did not matter to him that she was on the outs with the entire town of Heavenly. He was the largest rancher in the area. If he and Suzanne married, the fine citizens of Heavenly would have no choice but to deal with her.

Slocum let out a snort of self-derision. What made him think Suzanne would marry him, even if he was rich? But there were other fine-looking ladies in town. That had been the first thing Slocum noticed when he had ridden into Heavenly. Most towns sported two or three women of marrying age, usually uglier than a mud fence. Although none of the women he had seen in town could hold a candle to Suzanne, they were hardly so ill-graced that they were forced to wear flour sacks over their heads.

Rich, important to the entire commerce of Middle Park,

married. None of those had been more than fleeting dreams for Slocum.

"Slocum, I want a word with you."

Turning, Slocum saw Colorado Pete stalking toward him. Every time Slocum had seen him lately, the man was angrier than before. Slocum wished he had been able to follow him and find where he had gone when Ryan took Jenks to the doctor after getting buffaloed by the rustlers. Suzanne Underwood had caused him to take a different road. While he wasn't inclined to look poorly on their meeting, he wished he knew more about where Colorado Pete Kelso went when he rode off. It certainly wasn't to round up strays or look after the herd.

"You finished patrolling the upper meadows?" Slocum asked.

"Got Ryan and Jenks out there to do it," Kelso said. He scowled so hard, the lines seemed to etch themselves permanently into his face, cutting fleshy arroyos around his eyes and furrowing his forehead better than any Kansas farmer could plow a line. "When are you sellin' the Bar-S?"

"I've been thinking on that very idea," Slocum said.

"If you sell it right away, we can split the take and me and the boys can move on before snowfall. It gits mighty cold here along the western slope."

"If I sell, it's not going to be right away. No reason I shouldn't take my time."

"What? You have to sell, Slocum. Like I said, the snow. The cold. We'd have to weather another long winter to git our share. That ain't right!"

"The Bar-S is mine to do with as I see fit," Slocum said. The more Kelso argued for him to sell, the more Slocum dug in his heels.

"You gotta sell."

"Why don't you go out there with Ryan and Jenks? Maybe take a couple of the other boys. See if you can't track down some of those rustlers." Slocum watched Kelso closely. The man's anger was already in full blow. If there had been any trace of guilt, it was well hidden.

Kelso sputtered and spun around to storm away. Slocum considered firing the top hand then and there. Ryan would make a better worker, but Slocum's pa had always told him to face his enemies so he wouldn't have to worry about his back. Calling Colorado Pete an enemy might be stretching things, but Slocum couldn't be sure.

Slocum waited for Kelso to ride out. It wasn't lost on him that the top hand left by himself. Standing on the corral rails, Slocum watched Kelso start for the high meadow, then abruptly veer away and head to the south. If he followed that trail, he would eventually circle back onto the main road into Heavenly.

Tracking Kelso seemed more productive of his time and effort than anything else. For all the work required to run the Bar-S, Slocum found himself at loose ends now and again. He preferred being out with the cattle, but owning the spread forced him to deal with all the cowboys and the paperwork, not to mention planning for the drive to the railhead and a dozen other things.

Unable to decide on another mount, he saddled the gelding and went directly for the main road. If Kelso doubled back toward Heavenly, he had to pass Slocum. If he went on south, Slocum could catch up in an hour or two and find where the wrangler went.

Slocum rolled himself a smoke and puffed silently on it, continuing his thoughts from when he had perched like a crow on a fence. This time he found it hard to focus. The more he tried to concentrate, the more chaotic his thoughts became. It was with some relief that he saw Kelso coming up the road, heading for town. From his vantage point, he watched until Kelso disappeared around a bend in the road.

Only then did Slocum start his slow pursuit. Kelso had been riding fast, but if he stayed on the road, Slocum would get to town an hour or so after him. That was plenty of time to have a drink and ask around. He could even find Doc Gainsborough and talk some with him. Of all the people interested in the Bar-S, Ben Gainsborough was the only one who had advised him not to sell. Somehow, Slocum doubted it was because the doctor had taken such a liking to him that he wanted him to stay.

Slocum rode past the cutoff going toward Seamus Murphy's spread. As he'd done so many times before, he would have kept riding, hardly noticing the narrow road winding back into the hills before opening onto the lush valley. This time, however, he drew rein and then dismounted to study the soft dirt at the edge of the road.

A narrow-wheeled buggy had cut down into the grass and left distinct tracks recently. Slocum rubbed along the side of the groove and watched it crumble. The buggy had come this way only an hour earlier—or less.

The only person he had seen driving a buggy in the area had come this way before—and once more traveled along the road. Slocum looked down the road toward Heavenly and then into the hills. He could always find Kelso later. Suzanne Underwood proved a more fascinating diversion for his tracking skills.

As he rode, he considered the possibility that he might talk with Seamus Murphy. The man's ranch lay somewhere farther along the road. Slocum wanted to know more about this part of the countryside. If he saw a few rustlers here, that might mean they had their hideout nearby. With the mountains unexpectedly rising and turning into odd valleys all over the landscape, the outlaws might hide about anywhere. But if they hid, they still had to move the stolen cattle to get paid for their crime. Slocum doubted Marshal Zamora would ever be bribed into allowing stolen cattle into Heavenly. Other towns were miles distant. It would pay for Slocum to explore a bit more and find out if the marshals and sheriffs in those towns were inclined to look the other way as herds of stolen cattle were sold.

He passed the spot where Suzanne had driven off the road that night. Then he came to his dead horse. The buzzards and bugs had almost picked the carcass clean. He patted the nervous gelding's neck and said, "Don't worry. That's not going to happen to you."

He brought the horse to a trot, then slowed after another half mile when voices drifted to him. It took him a while to locate the source. Two people stood under a scrub oak fifty yards off the road. Even at this distance he could tell they argued by the way their arms flailed about. He didn't need the field glasses in his saddlebags to know one of them was Suzanne. Her skirt flared as she turned from side to side and raised her hand high. She shoved the man back a step, but he did not retaliate.

Slocum heard their muffled argument but could not figure what the fight was about. He reached back, pulled out his binoculars, and brought them up to get a better look at the man.

Somehow, he was not surprised to see Seamus Murphy. The young rancher whirled about, his back to Suzanne, and faced Slocum's direction. She shoved him again but Murphy stood stolidly, arms crossed on his chest and looking as if he had been carved from stone.

To ride closer, Slocum would have to reveal himself. That wouldn't be too bad because Suzanne and Murphy were about at the end of their argument. Her pose duplicated the man's. They stood back to back, arms crossed and now silent. Slocum lowered the field glasses and tucked them back into his saddlebags. Slowly, he urged his horse toward the pair.

He had no warning as a bullet tore through his pants leg. The slug was quickly followed by another and another, and Slocum was falling to the ground.

12

The gelding jerked to the side and reared, throwing Slocum to the ground. He landed hard enough to knock the wind from his lungs. Through the bloodred haze cloaking his eyes, he saw the horse stagger away. He lay still, struggling to regain his wind. The pain subsided. Careful tensing and relaxing of his muscles convinced Slocum he had not broken a rib falling, no matter how much it felt like it with every breath he sucked in. Turning his head slowly, he tried to find where the sniper who had shot him lay hidden. The best cover lay a couple dozen yards off the road in a clump of weeds.

Hand moving gradually, he slid over his belly and wrapped his fingers around the butt of his Colt Navy. He waited for any movement, but nothing came. When he was sure he was strong enough, he jerked to his right and then rolled left as fast as he could to end up in the shallow ditch beside the road. Slocum wiggled along on his belly until he got closer to the weeds. He reared up, six-shooter clutched in his hand. He was still shaken from the fall, but his hand was steady enough to fire.

If there had been a target, he would have squeezed off a shot. All he saw were broken weeds where the rifleman had

lain in wait for him. He got to his feet and approached war-
ily. The ground was hard enough to make tracking by boot
prints difficult. He found a spent, shiny brass shell casing.
Other than this, he saw nothing. Whoever had ambushed
him had lit out like his ass was on fire.

Slocum slid his six-gun back into its holster and then
looked for his horse. His heart almost exploded when he saw
the horse on its front knees, struggling to stand. Hurrying
over, he saw that the bullet tearing through his pants leg had
gone into the gelding's side. Pink froth came from the
horse's nostrils. Slocum drew his six-shooter and fired a
single shot into the horse's head. It let out a cry of pain and
surprise before dying.

"Damn you," Slocum cried. "That's the second horse of
mine you've killed! I swear, you'll pay for it!" He looked
around for any trace of the unseen gunman, but he might as
well have been the only human in a dozen miles.

Then he remembered what had lured him in this direction
in the first place. Suzanne Underwood and Seamus Murphy
had been arguing not a hundred yards away. Trudging through
the weeds, he reached the small stand of junipers and looked
around, but they were gone. One set of hoofprints headed due
east. He followed the small footprints that had to be Suzanne's
to a spot where she had climbed into her buggy and driven off.
Any help he might have gotten from either of them had evaporated.

Trudging back to his dead horse, he stripped off the saddle
and other tack, heaved them onto his shoulder, and started
back for his ranch house. It got farther every time.

When Slocum returned to the Bar-S ranch house, all the
hands were gone. He reckoned they were out tending the
herd and getting it rounded up for moving to the railhead.
This was an especially dangerous time for both the cowboys
and the herd. Rustlers could kill several cowboys in a simple
ambush and not have to work to round up most of the cattle.

That sort of worry could wait. Slocum was dog tired. He

dropped his gear on the front porch and went inside to find a pitcher and some water. He gulped the water straight from the pitcher and then splashed water on his face to get some of the dust off. Only then did he realize how tired he was. His feet hurt something fierce and his legs threatened to snap under him like toothpicks.

He went into Wimmer's study—*his* study now—and sank down into the chair where the old rancher had died. Slocum leaned back and closed his eyes, but he opened them slowly to stare at the bullet hole in the ceiling. It was fresh. He could tell because the wood splinters around the hole were not discolored. How it had come to be there was beyond him since only one round had been fired from the six-shooter found on the floor.

Seamus Murphy's six-gun.

Slocum closed his eyes and started to drift to sleep. Something niggled at the back of his mind, like a feather tickling his throat, but it went away when he heard the front door creaking open. In one smooth motion that belied his tiredness, he was on his feet, six-shooter drawn and pointed at the door of the study as . . . Suzanne Underwood came in.

"Oh," she said, her hand going to her mouth. "I didn't mean to startle you."

"It could be deadly," he said, returning the pistol to its place on his left hip. "Do you always barge in without knocking?"

"But I did knock. Twice. Didn't you hear me? When I found the door open, I thought I'd come in and—"

"And?" Slocum saw a sly look come to her bright blue eyes.

"And see if I might talk to you."

"Talk?"

"It's something we haven't done much of," Suzanne said. "Not that I mind."

"Seems we had plenty of chance to talk," Slocum said. "And a mite more."

"Oh, John, it was hardly what I'd call 'a mite more.' It was a considerable amount more."

Slocum tried to read something in the young woman's face and couldn't do it. Her eyes fixed on him like a snake following a bird, but there was no lust there. Discounting what she said, he tried to figure out why she had actually come to the Bar-S.

"I was riding earlier, hunting for strays," he said. "I thought I saw you and Seamus Murphy talking."

"Did you now?"

"More like you were arguing. How is it you know Murphy?"

"Who doesn't know him? For all the miles of rangeland, the area around Heavenly is mighty small. Or should I say, there aren't many folks on it."

"You mosey about a lot," Slocum said. "What is it that brings you out my way?"

Again he saw the light in her eyes, but it wasn't for him. Not exactly. He wondered if there was any way Seamus Murphy could have been the shooter. If so, that meant Suzanne knew about the man's murderous ways since she could not have ridden away fast enough to avoid seeing the attack. He had seen her and the rancher together, then been shot at. Slocum shook his head. Unless Murphy was made of smoke, he could never have reached the patch of weeds fast enough where the sniper had lain in wait.

"You're shaking your head, John? Are you telling me to leave? That you don't want my company?"

"Seems like me and Murphy are about the only two in the whole of Colorado who want your company," he said. The way she reared back like he had struck her told him he had touched a nerve.

"That's not a nice thing to say."

"But it's true," he said.

"They don't approve of my upbringing." Suzanne stood stiffly, eyes fixed on the far wall where no picture hung. The play of emotion told Slocum she was reliving an unpleasant past. "My pa was not very likable, and he treated me like dirt."

"Seems that would make folks cotton more to you."

"My pa," she went on, as if she had not heard, "threw my ma and me out. Drove us off like we were nothing more than dogs. Nobody in town would have anything to do with us because he would have taken it out on them if they had helped." A sneer came to Suzanne's lovely lips. "They're all cowards, each and every last one of them. I hate them as much as I do my pa, but for a different reason. I hate him for what he was and them for what they aren't." The words were cold and flat, and warned Slocum to drop the question. Whatever bad blood there was between her and the citizens of Heavenly had to remain hidden. For a while longer. Slocum could and not imagine how the entire town could turn against a woman and her daughter after being turned out by a tyrant.

Before Slocum could say another word, he heard the pounding of hooves outside. He swung around and faced the door as Ryan burst in, out of breath and face red from exertion.

"Mr. Slocum, you gotta come quick like a fox. We caught 'em. We caught a whole damned passel of 'em."

"Rustlers?"

"Must be six or eight of 'em. Shot it out with a couple, winged one. Got some more trapped in a box canyon."

"You can stay if you like," Slocum said to Suzanne. He was not certain if he wanted her to be here when he returned, but she settled the matter.

Stiffly, she said, "I will not remain here one instant longer." Suzanne spun and flounced off. Ryan started to say something, then looked at Slocum and clamped his mouth shut.

"Let's ride," Slocum said. He pushed past Ryan and hefted his gear on the way to the corral. A quick look at the horses nervously moving about there convinced him a dun mare was his best choice. In minutes, he had saddled and ridden after an anxious cowhand.

"Tell me what happened," Slocum said.

"It was like this, Mr. Slocum. Me and the others was rounding up the cattle when they tried shootin' it out with us. They didn't know four more of us was on the way back to camp. We outnumbered 'em two to one. Lead flew and horses were rearin' and—"

"Anyone hurt?"

"None of us, Mr. Slocum. No, sir, we surprised them outlaws and even winged one of them. They lit out with us on their tails. Drove 'em into Blue Rock Canyon. You know the one?"

Slocum didn't and said so.

"Box canyon. Colorado Pete, he chased 'em and then stopped when he got to the mouth to wait for us. When we get enough firepower, we kin go on in and flush 'em."

Slocum frowned. Colorado Pete Kelso wasn't the sort of man he expected to lead the attack against the rustlers. If anything, he would hang back and let others, like Ryan and his partner, take the lead—and the bullets.

They rode hard for twenty minutes before Slocum heard sporadic gunfire. From the sound, only a couple men were firing.

"Sounds like we got ourselves a fight goin' on," Ryan said. He licked his lips and looked apprehensive.

"You ever kill a man?"

"No, sir, I never have, and that's the gospel truth. Gives me the willies thinkin' 'bout it, but ever since Jenks got his head bashed in, it's been worryin' at me like a burr under a saddle blanket."

"You'd kill to save Jenks?"

"Reckon so. And 'bout any of the rest of the boys. They're a good crew, Mr. Slocum."

"Keep your pistol in its holster unless you've got something worth shooting at," Slocum said. He galloped ahead and drew rein near Jenks. The man was bent over in pain, but he looked as eager as Ryan to get on with capturing himself some rustlers.

"Colorado Pete's got 'em all bottled up," Jenks said.

"You shouldn't be riding yet," Slocum said. "Didn't Doc Gainsborough tell you to put in some bunk time?"

"Cain't make money layin' about," Jenks said. Bandages that had been white once poked out from under his Stetson, giving mute testimony to his earlier injury.

More gunfire from within the canyon echoed out. Slocum's keen ear picked out only one six-shooter firing.

"How many rustlers are in there?"

"Cain't tell, but Colorado Pete's gone after 'em."

This struck Slocum as odd, but he might have misjudged Kelso entirely.

"You watch the mouth of the canyon. Don't shoot just because someone's coming out—it might be me or Kelso. If it's not us, try to capture them."

"How hard?" Ryan asked.

"Not so hard you put your lives in danger," Slocum said. He snapped the reins and moved his horse onto the narrow trail leading into Blue Rock Canyon. As he entered, he saw why it had gotten the name. The rocks weren't blue, but had a greenish tint to them that would appear blue near sundown. He wasn't much of a geologist, but there might be turquoise in the canyon walls, or maybe copper ore.

Several shots came in rapid succession, then nothing. Slocum galloped ahead, reaching for his six-gun as he rode. Not twenty yards ahead he saw that Kelso had the drop on a man half hidden by vegetation.

"Kelso, don't shoot him!"

Slocum's sharp command caused Colorado Pete Kelso to jerk around. His pistol rose, as if he intended to fire on Slocum. Then he swung back and aimed.

"He's surrendering, Kelso. Don't shoot a man with his

hands in the air or, I swear, I'll see you in jail for murder!" As much as Slocum wanted to end the miserable life of every single rustler in central Colorado, he wanted this one alive. Dead men couldn't give him information about where the rustlers camped or how many head they might have made off with already. Even more important, Slocum wanted to know how many outlaws he faced.

"He's a low-down, no-account sidewinder," Kelso said. He aimed and was going to fire, but Slocum rode forward and then jerked hard on the reins, causing the dun mare to dig in her heels. A cloud of dust rose between the cowboy and the rustler.

"Damn it, Slocum, I had him."

"He's not going anywhere," Slocum said. He saw a dead horse off in the brush. Some of the earlier gunfire had claimed yet another animal. If this kept up, there wouldn't be a single cowboy in all of Middle Park astride a horse.

"He ambushed me," the man in the brush called. "He opened fire on me and there was no call for him to do that!"

"He's a rustler," Kelso said, moving to get a shot.

Slocum dropped to the ground and drew his Colt Navy. This brought Kelso around when he saw who the six-shooter was aimed at—and it wasn't the rustler in the bushes.

"You got the wrong damn man in your sights, Slocum."

"Put the gun in your holster, Kelso." Slocum waited until the top hand reluctantly obeyed. Only then did Slocum turn and call to the hidden man. "You come on out. Keep those hands grabbing clouds."

The man slowly came from shadow and stepped into the sunlight angling down over the canyon rim.

"You shoulda let me shoot him, Slocum," said Kelso.

"I'm no rustler."

"You've got a powerful lot of explaining to do," Slocum said to Seamus Murphy. The young rancher glared at him, but had the good sense to keep his hands high in the air.

13

"You got no right to hold me," Seamus Murphy said. His jaw thrust out and his eyes flashed angrily. The instant he started to lower his hands, Kelso reached for his gun again.

Slocum moved fast, grabbing Kelso's wrist to keep him from drawing.

"We got him," Slocum said. "Back off."

"You're the one what wanted rustlers cut down. This is one of the worst. We caught him red-handed."

"What are you doing on Bar-S land?" Slocum watched Murphy closely. Somehow, he could not believe the young rancher was out rustling. He was such a hothead, he wouldn't last ten minutes with a gang. He would anger the wrong outlaw and get shot in the back. The only possibility was that Murphy was hunting for strays to move to his own herd. Even a few cattle from the Bar-S herd might mean the difference between surviving and having to turn his ranch over to the bank in foreclosure.

"Some of my cattle strayed here. I was lookin' for 'em."

"Liar! You were stealin' Bar-S beeves!"

"Shut up, Kelso," Slocum said. "He might be telling the truth." If Slocum expected any gratitude from Murphy, he would have been wrong. Murphy glared at him as hard as he did at Colorado Pete Kelso.

"Go on, murder me. You won't believe anything I have to say. String me up! That'll make you feel good, won't it? You can brag on it around Heavenly."

"Let Marshal Zamora sort it all out." Slocum waved to Jenks and Ryan, who had ridden up and watched in silence. "Get him into town and tell the marshal what happened."

"I'll go with them. They'll let this bastard get away, sure as the sun rises." Kelso's fingers tapped on the butt of his pistol.

"Go on," Slocum said. "And you," he said directly to Kelso, "get on back to finding rustlers. We're too close to rounding up the herd for them to bother us now."

Kelso spat at Murphy, swung around, and stalked to his horse. He jumped into the saddle and galloped off.

Slocum watched Ryan and Jenks ride off on either side of a defiant Seamus Murphy, then turned his attention to the trail taken by Kelso. He wondered if Suzanne Underwood waited back at the ranch house, but he doubted it. She had acted as if every step into the house had been barefoot over hot coals. Slocum wondered if it was a coincidence that Suzanne had shown up about the time Murphy was out riding on Bar-S rangeland. He shrugged it off. He had something else eating at him even more.

Once out of the box canyon, he stepped down from his horse and examined the ground for traces of Kelso's horse. Wherever Kelso rode, it wasn't back to the high meadow where most of the herd milled about, waiting for the cowboys to move them north. Slocum found the trail and followed it cautiously.

After twenty minutes, he caught sight of Colorado Pete ahead. He halted and reached for his field glasses. It took a few seconds for him to figure out what he was seeing. Kelso remained on his horse some distance from a ravine. Movement at the edge of the ravine caught Slocum's attention, and he sat a little straighter when he caught sight of the crowns of two battered hats. Kelso talked with the men hiding in the deep arroyo, but Slocum could not get a good look at them other than to see that one hat had a cut alongside the crown and that it had, at one time, been a bright Kelly green. Sun and wind had faded it to a shade Slocum could not put a name to. After five minutes, Slocum lowered the binoculars and tucked them away, never having seen the faces of the men in the ravine. Kelso rode off, heading due west.

Slocum waited, hoping to catch sight of the men who had remained hidden, but they used the steep banks to mask their departure. Slocum could not even tell which way they left. He considered tracking them, but knew he would be stirring up a hornet's nest. If he poked around too much by himself, he was sure to run afoul of what had to be a new gang of rustlers. He had been the target of too many rustlers' ambushes since coming to Colorado.

Retracing his trail, Slocum came to the fork in the road, one branch leading to the Bar-S ranch house and the other to Heavenly. He chose to ride into town.

It was after dark by the time he reached Heavenly. He licked his lips and tasted dust, but rather than head for the Prancing Pony and Gutherie's quick pour from a bottle of decent whiskey, he went to the marshal's office.

"What you want, Slocum?"

"Pleased to see you, too, Marshal," Slocum said. He dropped to the ground and wrapped the reins around a hitching post.

"Don't go thinking you own the town."

"What gossip have you been listening to?" Slocum faced him squarely.

"What do you want, Slocum?"

"My boys brought in Seamus Murphy. You have him locked up inside?" Slocum waited as Marshal Zamora thought on the matter before nodding once. "You mind if I talk to him?" Zamora shook his head. "Thanks, Marshal."

Slocum pushed past the lawman and went into the small office. A pair of cages at the rear were empty. The third held an angry, pacing, cursing Seamus Murphy. The rancher looked up sharply when Slocum came closer.

"What do you want? To put the noose around my neck?" Murphy reached up and tugged at the orange bandanna he wore. He slid a finger under it and lifted, mocking the way a noose would tighten.

"That what's going on in town?" Slocum grabbed a chair and pulled it where he could sit down and look at Murphy. "They going to lynch you?"

"You put me in here," Murphy said. "It's all your fault."

"The way folks think about you has nothing to do with me," Slocum said. "Why do they hate you so much?"

"Go to hell."

"Does it have something to do with Suzanne Underwood?" Slocum wished he were playing poker with Murphy. The expression on the rancher's face was too easy to read. "Why does everyone in Heavenly hate her? For all that, why does she hate *them*?"

"You leave her out of this. The marshal's the one talkin' 'bout charging me with Wimmer's murder."

Slocum considered this and discounted it. Zamora must have thrown that into the stew pot to get Murphy to confess to something else. Rustling cattle was nowhere near as bad as murder, though both might get a man strung up.

"Unless the marshal thinks I'm in cahoots with you, I gave you an alibi for the time Wimmer was killed." Slocum remembered how Marshal Zamora had toyed with this notion. If the lawman had moved on, giving in to facts rather than reflexive dislike for Murphy, all that had to be dealt with were the rustling charges.

"Why'd you bother? You hate me like the rest of these . . ."

Murphy began sputtering incoherently. His anger was so great, he couldn't even think up an appropriate insult. Considering the colorful language Slocum had heard as he came into the jail, that was almost unbelievable.

"I like to know the truth. You were drinking with me when Wimmer was shot. But that doesn't mean Suzanne Underwood might not have something to do with it." Slocum remained impassive as Murphy smashed hard against the iron bars, fingers groping for Slocum's throat.

"You get back or I swear I'll shoot you like a weasel in a trap," Marshal Zamora roared. Slocum had not heard the lawman open the outer door. He pointed his six-shooter directly at Murphy to make him obey.

"There's no call to shoot a man already in jail," Slocum said. He doubted anything more would come from Murphy's lips but curses. Without another word, he left the jailhouse, stepping into the cool Colorado night.

Slocum took a few seconds to wonder why he didn't leave Murphy to his fate, much of it caused by the young rancher's own hotheaded deeds. He could do that, but it wouldn't be right. With some reluctance, he passed the open doors of the Prancing Pony and the gaiety inside and headed down a side street until he reached Ben Gainsborough's office. He knocked on the door.

"Why, good evening, Mr. Slocum." Nora Gainsborough held the door as if she expected to slam it, and relaxed only when she saw him.

"Were you expecting someone?"

"Ben's out on a call. Mrs. Fiarino's having a baby any time now."

"Mind if I come in?"

She had relaxed, but now she tensed and looked as if she wanted to bolt and run. "No, come on in. Could I get you some coffee?"

"That'd be fine." Slocum doubted a cup of coffee, even if Nora Gainsborough fixed it to perfection, would do anything to cut his real thirst. Whiskey would do that, not coffee. He settled down in a chair and watched as she bustled about, reaching for a coffeepot on the Franklin stove at the side of the office.

"Tell me about Seamus Murphy," Slocum said as she turned with two cups. She hesitated, then handed one cup to Slocum.

"Why do you think I know anything about him?"

"Nobody in town will talk about him or Suzanne Underwood."

"Is that so? I know nothing about them that would interest you."

"All sorts of things interest me," Slocum said, sipping at the coffee. He nodded in her direction to show his approval. He had drunk better coffee, but it still went down well. "I wouldn't mind hearing about Jackson Wimmer either." This time she could not maintain her stony facade. Her lips thinned and the vein on her left temple began pulsing visibly.

"It's no secret that I found the man despicable. Most all in town did. He was crude, had a sharp tongue, and did not mind sharing his low opinion of all things living with anyone unable to escape quickly enough."

"Being the richest man in Middle Park gave him license to say anything he wanted?"

"The way he treated people, he could have been the richest man in the whole world and it wouldn't have been right. I'm surprised someone didn't take a gun to him earlier."

"Do you think Suzanne Underwood might have been capable of shooting a man like Wimmer?"

Nora Gainsborough sat straighter and put her cup down on a low table.

"It's time for you to leave, Mr. Slocum. Mind you, I bear you no ill will because Jackson Wimmer chose to give you the Bar-S. My tolerance for discussing him is very small."

"Sorry if I offended you, Mrs. Gainsborough," Slocum

said. "One thing you could probably answer. How did the ranch come to be named the Bar-S?"

If Slocum thought she had been pissed off before, now he saw hatred in her eyes. He couldn't tell if it was directed at him or Wimmer or even someone else.

"I cannot comment on that. Good evening, sir."

She opened the door and tapped her foot waiting for him to leave.

As Slocum started to leave, he almost bumped into Ben Gainsborough. The doctor wore a smile ear to ear.

"Slocum, good to see you." Gainsborough looked past and said to Nora, "It was a girl. She's naming it Catherine Marie. Both mother and daughter are doing fine, though the baby's a little on the light side, but it was a difficult pregnancy." Gainsborough dropped his medical bag by the door and slapped Slocum on the shoulder. "Join me in a drink. That's why you came by, isn't it?"

"Ben, he—" Nora Gainsborough chewed her lower lip and looked uneasy.

"I have to be on my way."

"One drink, Slocum. Good whiskey. Special bottle. I keep it for celebrations."

"I don't know that a baby being born is such a thing to celebrate," Slocum said.

"You sound positively Irish. Cry at births, laugh at funerals. Well, I'm not Irish and I want to celebrate my upcoming marriage."

Slocum stared at Gainsborough, thinking he had misheard him. He glanced at Nora Gainsborough and then back. Her expression was unreadable.

"Whose marriage?" he asked.

"Mine and Nora's. I thought that was why you came by, to congratulate us."

"But you're married already. I don't follow what you're saying." Slocum saw the flash of confusion on Gainsborough's face as he held out a water tumbler generously filled with whiskey. Hardly realizing he did so, Slocum took it. He kept his eyes fixed on the doctor.

"You aren't a local, so you didn't know. Nora and I, well, we haven't gotten married. We just shared a roof."

"And a bed," Nora Gainsborough said sharply. "There's no need to be coy. We've lived as husband and wife. We finally decided to make it legal."

Slocum started to ask if there wasn't a judge or preacher in town, but he knew there were two ministers. For whatever reason, they had not chosen to marry.

"Congratulations," Slocum said, thrusting out his hand. Gainsborough shook it. "I shouldn't have called you Mrs. Gainsborough," he said to Nora, "but I thought . . ."

"That's all right. You're new to town and no reason for you to inquire."

"How long?" Slocum bit off the question. It was none of his business.

"A few years," Nora said quickly.

"Why now?" Slocum asked. "If things were working for you as it was, why tie the knot?"

"I finally decided to make an honest woman of her," Gainsborough said, looking at Nora. Slocum saw her looking daggers at him, and knew there wouldn't be an explanation beyond what he had gotten.

"When's the shindig?" he asked.

"We'll set a date in a few days," Gainsborough said. "There's a lot of planning to do."

"There's very little remaining to do," Nora said. "I've had it planned ever since . . . for years."

Slocum considered all the couple said and couldn't make head nor tail of it.

"This isn't much, but it ought to go a ways toward your wedding," Slocum said. "What do I owe you for patching up Jenks?"

"No charge," Gainsborough said, obviously too happy with delivering a healthy baby and telling Slocum of his upcoming nuptials, but Nora had no such qualms.

"No charge for rooming for the day he spent here," she said quickly. "Five dollars for bandaging him up."

"Sounds reasonable," Slocum said, fishing in his vest pocket. He found four single dollar bills and added a silver cartwheel to the pile on the table beside his coffee cup. "I hope I don't have to pay you any more for repairing my cowboys."

"From what I hear, you just might," Doc Gainsborough said. "Going after the rustlers the way you are is going to cause lead to fly."

"I'll keep my head down," Slocum promised. He touched the brim of his hat in Nora Gainsborough's direction and then downed the remainder of the whiskey in his glass. He left quickly.

The door shut behind him and he heard Nora's muffled voice rising in anger. Slocum wondered what had sparked it, but if he had to bet, he would place all his money on his visit and the questions asked about Seamus Murphy—and Suzanne Underwood.

It was time for him to get a few more whiskeys under his belt. He headed for the Prancing Pony and a half bottle of Gutherie's best liquor.

14

Slocum settled down with his bottle of whiskey at the corner of the Prancing Pony bar so he could watch the sporadic coming and going of the patrons. Gutherie enthusiastically served four cowboys from another spread, keeping them drinking by reciting any of a dozen timeworn tall tales. He was more comfortable here than he ever had been in the general store. While it might have something to do with the whiskey Gutherie sampled now and then, Slocum reckoned the man preferred the company in the bar to that of the store.

Letting the liquor slide down his gullet and puddle warmly helped Slocum think on what had been said over at Doc Gainsborough's office. The more he thought, the more he realized that other citizens of Heavenly skirted Nora Gainsborough—or whatever her name was. They had to deal with the doctor and tolerated her, but they did not shun her the way they did Seamus Murphy or Suzanne Underwood. For all the initial friendly appearances when he had ridden into Heavenly, Slocum realized now that the undercurrent in the town was one of suspicion and outright scorn. What Suzanne and Murphy had done to earn it, he was at a loss to say. An unmarried woman living in sin certainly explained everyone's attitude toward Nora.

He knocked back another shot and stared at the door. For a moment, he thought the whiskey had clouded his vision. Then he sat straighter and stared hard. His eyesight was as sharp as an eagle's. Moving back and forth just above the tall swinging doors, a tall-brimmed hat captured his attention completely. He had seen that hat before, with a notch cut out of the crown and a peculiar color green.

"One of the men Kelso was talking to, the one hidden down in the ravine," Slocum said aloud. Two gamblers at the next table glanced in his direction, then hastily turned back to their game when he glared at them.

He picked up his bottle, still sloshing with a good six or eight drinks left, and set it down on the bar.

"Gutherie, do me a favor and save this for the next time I come in."

"Sure thing, Mr. Slocum. It's got your name on it," the bar owner said jovially. From the way he worked the four cowboys bellied up to the bar, he was having a profitable night and no request would have been too outrageous. The usual way would have been for Slocum to take the bottle with him or simply leave it. Any number of other bar patrons would have pounced on it the instant he left. Saving it for later was a service that no barkeep wanted to catch on.

Slocum was out the swinging doors and looking around before Gutherie recorked the bottle and stashed it on the back bar. Slocum looked up and down the main street. A slow smile came to his lips. In front of the darkened barbershop, Kelso and the man with the peculiar hat pressed close together, whispering. If ever he had seen men up to no good, it was these two.

When they hurried off, Slocum found his horse and mounted. He waited a few minutes to be sure they weren't riding toward him, then headed down the street in the direction they had taken. He urged his horse to a long trot, and soon spotted the riders ahead. From this distance in the dark, he couldn't be sure he followed Kelso and the man wearing the cut-up green hat, but who else would be out for a nocturnal ride?

The riders cut off the road and headed into the hills. For more than an hour Slocum followed, falling back when he had to be sure they did not spot him. When he caught the scent of a campfire and cooking beef, he slowed and eventually stepped down from his horse and advanced on foot.

In a hollow, six men crouched around a fire, helping themselves to sizzling steaks. Slocum didn't have to see anymore to know where that beef had come from. The six were on Bar-S land, and in the distance he heard the mournful lowing of cattle. His cattle. He had found another gang of rustlers.

Before he retreated, he spied on them, trying to identify Colorado Pete Kelso. When he realized it wasn't possible in the dark, Slocum reluctantly left, found his horse, and galloped back toward town. He was out of the saddle and running a few steps when he reached the jailhouse.

He tried the door, but it was locked.

"Marshal! Marshal Zamora! Let me in. I found some rustlers."

He heard grumbling inside the jail. The bar locking the door scraped free and a crack appeared. Both a bloodshot eye and the barrel of a shotgun poked out.

"I tracked down a half dozen rustlers," Slocum said. "They're bedded down for the night by now not all that far away. Get a posse and we can catch them red-handed."

"Damnation, Slocum, don't you ever sleep? I busted up a fight tonight and sent two cowboys back to their spread, flat on their backs in a wagon."

Slocum stood his ground. The marshal could not simply return to bed. Zamora grumbled some more, opened the door, and motioned for Slocum to come in.

"Lemme get my pants on. Six of the varmints, you say?"

"A couple hours' ride from here, right on the edge of the Bar-S."

"So they stole your beeves? You offerin' a reward?"

"You can't claim any reward."

"Not for me. Who in their right mind's gonna traipse out in the middle of the night after outlaws likely to ventilate them 'less there's money on the line?"

"Twenty dollars for every man," Slocum said, realizing the lawman was right.

"That's a princely sum. Sure you want to go that high?"

"I want to make certain no rustler thinks of the Bar-S as easy prey."

"Not that, not since you showed up. You've done a right good job of running them bastards to ground—or stringing them up," Zamora said. He opened a drawer and grabbed a box of shells for his shotgun. "You get on outta here while I round up some men."

Slocum glanced into the cell where Seamus Murphy lay. Murphy was not asleep, but he wasn't sociable enough not to pretend to be asleep.

Slocum left, Zamora right behind him. The lawman started to say something, then thought better of it. Insulting Slocum by suggesting he was leading them on a wild-goose chase to break Murphy out of jail wouldn't accomplish anything.

Slocum mounted, and waited impatiently for the marshal and four men to join him. From the way the four wobbled in the saddle, he guessed Zamora had found them all in a saloon.

"Will they be sober enough when we get there?" Slocum looked at them and wondered if a couple might not fall out of the saddle before they left Heavenly.

"Only way to find out is to get there," Zamora said. "Lead the way, Slocum."

Because of the drunks, it took closer to three hours for Slocum to get back to the spot where he had spied on the rustlers' camp earlier in the evening. The fire had died down and six dark shapes were arrayed around it.

"Nobody on guard?"

"Don't see anyone," Slocum said. He elbowed the marshal when a cow let out a mournful cry.

"That's good enough for me. If those aren't your boys, then they're moving cattle across your land. Trespassing at the least."

Slocum was glad to see that the combination of the cold night ride and the sudden fear of the outlaws had sobered the four men with them. Two waited nervously while Zamora went with another in one direction and Slocum circled with the remaining posse member. Walking softly, he made his way down the slope into the outlaw camp. Slocum drew his six-shooter and waited for his partner to catch up. The man's hand shook as he held his own six-gun.

"I ain't never kilt nobody."

"No need to start tonight. If shooting starts, get under cover and stay there. Don't even think of firing your gun," Slocum cautioned. He knew he would be safer with only rustlers shooting at him. A frightened man behind him was likely to kill him by accident.

Slocum walked with a confident stride into the middle of the camp. He saw Zamora and the other newly deputized drunkard coming from the other direction.

"You're all under arrest for rustling," Slocum shouted.

The sleeping men stirred, then sat bolt upright. One went for a six-gun. Slocum kicked it away and covered the man. The others had even less presence of mind, being awakened from a sound sleep.

"Tie 'em up. Make sure the ropes are secure," Zamora ordered. The marshal snorted and shook his head. "So much for the wicked sleeping with an uneasy head. We could have taken the cattle back and they'd never have known."

Slocum saw the four deputies were feeling their oats now, pushing the rustlers around and acting like cocks of the walk.

"I want to see the cattle," Slocum said.

"Me, too. Hate to think I nabbed innocent men."

"Whoever they are, they're not innocent," Slocum said. And as they went down into the arroyo where close to twenty head of cattle were penned, he saw the Bar-S brand on more than one rump.

"Whose brand is this?" Slocum ran his fingers over the brand. "Looks like Circle M."

Zamora spat and said, "Murphy. That's Murphy's brand."

Slocum peered at the marshal through the dark; then a slight smile came to his lips.

"So he might have been telling the truth about hunting for his cattle on my land."

"He's rotten through and through."

"Disagreeable?"

"That," Zamora agreed.

"Just like Jackson Wimmer?"

"Get his damned cattle cut from your herd. I'll release the son of a bitch and tell him where he can find his beeves."

"I'll get my men to run the Bar-S cattle back into the pasture. I'll drive these back to Murphy myself."

"He doesn't appreciate anything anyone does for him."

Slocum said nothing to that as he made his way through the herd, swatting bovine rumps and forcing six cattle branded Circle M away from the rest. Nobody in Heavenly had done much for Murphy to appreciate. Even if they had, Murphy was not the sort to appreciate it. Slocum reflected on how it took a man a considerable amount of practice to accept generosity from others.

Like driving the six cows back onto Circle M land.

Slocum saw that the four deputies had their prisoners bound and on horseback, ready for the trip back to Heavenly. He studied each face closely, but Kelso was not among them. He stopped in front of the man with the faded green hat.

"You aren't rustling all by your lonesome. Who's helping you?"

"My partners here. Nobody else."

Slocum knew he had no way of forcing the man to talk. The man in the green hat was hardly the brains of a gang, but how much did it take to gather a few drifters together to rustle cattle? Figuring out an innocent reason for Kelso to meet twice with rustlers proved more than he could dream up on the spur of the moment.

"There might be others," Slocum told Marshal Zamora. "Keep a close eye on these six."

"Nobody's getting out of my jail unless I let them out," the marshal vowed. Slocum hoped Zamora wasn't blowing smoke.

The posse rode off with the prisoners while Slocum started Murphy's cattle on a trail leading toward the spot where he reckoned a ranch house might be situated. The cattle wanted to dawdle, and Slocum was half asleep in the saddle. It had been a hell of a long day, he hadn't eaten, and the whiskey sloshing in his belly made him a tad giddy. Still, knowing he had gotten Murphy out of jail and had even found the reason for the man prowling around on Bar-S land satisfied him.

Just before sunrise, he ran the cattle up to a small one-room cabin set in the middle of a stand of junipers. Murphy had done a fair job in proving his land. A small vegetable garden behind the cabin showed he had a little talent as a farmer, but his barn consisted of nothing more than a lean-to.

As Slocum shooed the cattle out to a pasture behind the cabin, he spotted a buggy still hitched up to its team. He rode closer, and noted that his repair work on Suzanne's buggy was holding up well. He tied his horse to the buggy frame and went to the cabin. From inside came sounds of things being thrown about.

Slocum drew his six-shooter and went to the door. He pushed it open with the toe of his boot. He lowered his gun when he saw Suzanne Underwood kneeling on the dirt floor, pawing through a box of clothing.

"You reckon Murphy has something that would fit you?"

Suzanne jumped as if he had touched her with a red-hot

poker. One hand went to her throat and the other burrowed about in the box.

"John! You startled me. What are you doing here?"

"I like that," he said.

She looked at him quizzically.

"The question you just asked. I like it so much I'm going to ask you the same one. What are *you* doing here? Robbing a man locked up in jail?"

"No, nothing of the sort." She struggled to find a plausible answer. "I was hunting for something that might exonerate him. Nobody in Heavenly likes him. They're going to railroad him, and I want to help."

"Because nobody in town likes you either?"

"Yes," she said. The word sounded as if a snake had spoken. It came out more as a hiss than a human sound.

"What would there be in there that would get him sprung from jail?"

"I don't know. That's why I was looking. A receipt perhaps, or a deed or something."

"He's not a rustler, but you know that," Slocum said, watching her reaction closely. Suzanne did a better job now of hiding whatever she felt. "I brought back a few head of his cattle that had gotten in with mine."

"You herded them back yourself?"

"Been a cowboy a long time," Slocum said, "and I know my way around a cow."

"That was mighty neighborly of you," she said. She licked her lips so that the pink tip of her tongue slid out and over her lips. Watching the small gesture caused emotions to stir within Slocum's loins. "Seems as if you ought to get a reward for that."

"Doing the right thing's reward enough," Slocum said. He knew he was lying. Suzanne was a lovely woman and he wanted more than the satisfaction of returning stolen cattle to their rightful owner. He wanted her.

Two sure steps took him across the room to her. His arm slipped around her waist and drew her in close. She molded easily to his body. Her eyelids drooped just a little as her lips opened. He kissed her.

One instant she had been pliant, almost boneless. Now she was more than an armful. She clutched him as hard as he was holding her. He felt her breasts mash down against his chest and her tongue come questing into his mouth. He let his hand drift lower until he could cup one firm buttock. He pulled her in even harder to his body. Her legs parted and she curled around one thigh where she began rubbing up and down faster and faster.

She broke off the kiss, panting hard. "I want more than this, John. I want you. In me. I want this."

He groaned as she gripped at his crotch and squeezed down. He was already hard. This made him want to explode.

"Wearing all these clothes isn't going to get either of us where we want to go," he said.

She moved her nimble fingers over his gun belt and let it fall to the dirt floor. Barely had it crashed down when she worked on the buttons of his fly. As she struggled to free his erection, he began working on her blouse. He caught his breath, as much from the feel of Suzanne's hand around his naked hardness as from the sight of her perfectly formed tits spilling from her blouse.

He bent over and kissed first one and then the other. Every time his tongue raked over the rubbery tip on each, she squeezed down hard on him. He had to struggle to keep from getting off too soon.

"Damn, but you're beautiful," he said as he buried his face between her breasts. He kissed and licked and then sucked in her left nipple to press against it with his tongue. This caused her to stumble a mite. Her grip on his manhood lessened as desire racked her trim body.

Slocum used the respite to slip off her blouse. She was

naked to the waist and this was not enough for him—for them. Together, they unfastened her skirt so she could step out of it. Clad now only in her high-button shoes, she was a vision of loveliness that made Slocum even more aware of how lucky he was.

"You're overdressed," she said accusingly. Working together again, they got Slocum's coat, vest, and shirt off. It took more work getting his pants off. He had to kick free of his boots for that.

"We're both as naked as jaybirds," she said. "Except for my shoes." She turned away from him, looked teasingly around as she bent to begin unbuttoning them.

"Don't bother," he said, moving in behind her. "I like the way you look, wearing nothing but them."

"How much do you like it?" Her voice was ragged with desire.

"This much," he said, stepping up so his crotch pressed into the firm roundness of her buttocks. He thrust forward between those half-moons and aimed down lower. He slipped along her nether lips and felt how ready she was. She reached back and caught at him, guiding him inside.

Slocum thought he was prepared for the slow entry into her core. He was wrong. It was new and wonderful and exciting as he slid slowly balls-deep into her tightness. He put his hands on her hips, but Suzanne lost her balance and rocked forward.

She caught herself on the edge of the bed and started to climb onto it.

"No, this way," Slocum said. Sweat beaded on his forehead now. He reached around so his forearm clamped firmly on her belly. With this for leverage, he pulled her back into his groin as he thrust forward. He had thought he was as deep as he could go. He was wrong. They both gasped in delight when, fully hidden, he began rotating his hips around. No spoon in a mixing bowl had ever felt finer or more fulfilled.

"Fast, John, do it faster. I want it hard."

"It's hard, all right." Slocum burned all the way down into

his balls. When Suzanne shoved her hips back as he drove forward, he knew he was losing control. He began pistoning faster, sinking deep and hot and hard.

He was vaguely aware of her crying out. He was too lost in his own sensations to notice. When he spilled his seed, he pulled her back into his crotch so hard he lost balance. They turned, still locked together, and he sat heavily on the bed where Suzanne had been leaning.

She straddled his legs as he sat, moving herself up and down furiously until there was no more reason to do so. Suzanne rolled to one side and finally crawled into the bed. Slocum lay half under her, feeling the sleek skin, her soft, hot breath, the way she moved lazily now.

"Will you, John?"

"Again? I'm plumb tuckered out. You do that to a man."

"Not that," she said, moving closer. He felt her still rigid nipples rubbing against his back as she scooted around. Her hand snaked over his body and worked lower to cradle his limp organ. One leg lifted over his so she could strop against his thigh.

"What then?"

"You'll help Seamus? He's in a world of trouble."

Slocum could only nod. He had done what he could to help the rancher—more than anyone else in Heavenly, he had done what he could. Somehow, he wasn't overly surprised that Suzanne wanted to help Murphy, too.

15

Slocum got back to the Bar-S ranch house by late afternoon the next day. He had spent a considerable amount of time with Suzanne Underwood, pleasurably so, but he felt a growing tension between them the longer they were together. Waiting at Murphy's small cabin for the man to return had not seemed a good idea, but Suzanne had insisted. Slocum wondered what Seamus Murphy's reaction would have been if he had found the two of them intimately engaged.

Shrugging it off since it never happened, Slocum went into the study and sank into Wimmer's chair. He heaved a deep sigh. This would always be Wimmer's chair since he had been sitting in it when he died. And this was Wimmer's office and, Slocum reluctantly admitted, the Bar-S was Wimmer's ranch. Jackson Wimmer had put his indelible brand on everything. Thought of selling it all off once the herd was sold and safely on railcars heading back East danced in Slocum's mind again.

Being tied down as a ranch owner didn't bother him as much as he thought it would. Inheriting the Bar-S worried at him in ways he had never considered, however. He had been *given* the ranch and had not earned it. The few weeks he had worked it as foreman hardly counted. Finding a twenty-dollar gold piece was one thing. Being handed a working, profitable ranch was another. It galled him that he saw no way of putting his own imprint on it. Even changing the name from Bar-S to something else made no sense. He could claim the brand as reasonable, him being Slocum and all. But Wimmer's Bar-S wasn't likely to ever be Slocum's Bar-S.

Even the notion of finding a filly in Heavenly and settling down faded after his tryst with Suzanne. None of the women in town could match her—and she wasn't going to let him throw a bridle on her and claim her as his own. He doubted any man could, but if one came close to getting her into his corral, it would be Seamus Murphy. Suzanne Underwood had never said as much, but Slocum knew she was sweet on the fiery Irishman.

He leaned back in the chair and stared at the bullet hole in the ceiling. Again came vague notions drifting across the edge of his mind like thistledown against his cheek. Just as quickly, the wind blew away any conclusion to the chaotic thoughts. Slocum reared back and clasped his hands behind his head. He looked around the spacious, well-appointed room, but for some reason his eyes came to rest on the blank wall to the side of the desk. This was the spot Suzanne had stared at so intently and that had caused such anger.

He groaned as he stood. He could ride all day and not feel this sore. Suzanne was a powerful lot of woman. Slocum went to the bare wall and looked closely at it. By catching the afternoon sun against the wall in just the right angle, he saw that a picture had hung here long enough for the wood around it to fade. A quick look around convinced him the picture had not been knocked down or otherwise fallen. Whatever had been here was gone.

Too many mysteries stalked the Bar-S for him to ever be comfortable here. Slocum came to his decision. He would sell the place after roundup. First, he needed to know what it was he was selling.

Going through the cabinets in the office revealed a ledger with Wimmer's crabbed writing and careful numbers all lined up in columns. Slocum dropped this onto the desk. He needed to study it and try to figure out how the old man had kept his books. If he wanted to sell the Bar-S, he needed to know exactly how profitable the place was and the full extent of the rangeland.

The rest of the cabinet revealed nothing of interest. Slocum moved to a low table just under the bare spot on the wall and found a drawer. He opened it and found a diary with Wimmer's name embossed on the cover in gold lettering. Slocum started to take it out, then stopped. Reading another's diary was worse than spying. Whatever Jackson Wimmer had thought would be recorded inside, Slocum wasn't sure he wanted to know. He hesitated again, then opened the cover. The diary dated back several years, making him wonder if there were earlier volumes all filled and filed somewhere. With sudden resolve, Slocum slammed shut the cover and pawed through the other items in the drawer. He had never thought Wimmer was the type to collect small broken wood toys and odd-colored rocks, but they were all in the drawer.

Slocum shut the drawer on Wimmer's peculiar treasures. There was only so much one man ought to know about another, and poking through this drawer gave him too much information about the crusty old galoot. The people in Heavenly might have hated Wimmer's guts, but Slocum had developed a certain respect for him, if not actual liking.

He had other matters to attend to instead of figuring out why Wimmer had saved the relics he had.

He pulled back the chair behind Wimmer's desk and sat. On the desk lay the ledger book taken from the cabinet, silently inviting him to use some skull sweat figuring out the financial details of the Bar-S. He rested his hand on the cover, and had started to open it when a pounding at the outer door echoed through the ranch house.

"Come on in," Slocum called. He leaned back. His hand drifted to his belt buckle so he could go for his six-shooter if trouble walked through the door.

Trouble like Colorado Pete Kelso.

Slocum was surprised to see his visitor was the gent from Heavenly.

"Slocum?" The man stood in the doorway, looking around as if he hunted for a rat hole to dive into.

"Mr. Robertson," Slocum said in greeting. He did not move his hand from the butt of his Colt Navy. "I didn't expect to see you again."

Rupert Robertson came into the room, eyes darting about suspiciously.

"You alone?"

"Only you and me, if that's what you call being alone," Slocum said. He rocked back, taking his hand from his pistol when he saw that Roop Robertson was not likely to gun him down. From what he could tell, the man was unarmed, though he might carry a small pistol in a shoulder rig. As Robertson approached, his jacket billowed out from his body. If he carried any weapon, it had to be up his sleeve or in his boot.

"I want the Bar-S. I'm willin' to pay up for it."

"It's not for sale." Slocum would have sold to Robertson if the man had come to him only ten minutes earlier. Or maybe not. Something about the weasel of a man irritated Slocum. He had no real bond to the Bar-S, but the ranch deserved to be in better hands than those of Roop Robertson.

"I'll offer you more 'n you could ever hope to get from anybody else."

"Who the hell are you?"

The question took Robertson by surprise. The man's mouth opened and closed like a trout flopped up on a riverbank. Robertson finally got his wits about him.

"Just a body who knows a value. The Bar-S is a good ranch. You're not the ownin' type."

"And you are?" Slocum looked the man over and knew, whatever Robertson did for a living, it was not ranching. The closest this potential buyer had ever come to a cow was sticking a fork in a steak at some restaurant. The more Slocum looked, the more he wondered if Robertson had ever had enough money to even buy a steak. His clothing was threadbare, his boots unpolished, and it might have been a while since he had eaten a square meal.

"'Course I am. I . . . I got plenty of money to buy the ranch off you."

Slocum stood and went around the large desk. Robertson backed away as he came. Even expecting Slocum to attack him, Robertson was too slow by half. Slocum grabbed the man by the throat and lifted until only his toes dragged along the carpet.

"Who are you working for? You don't have two nickels to rub together, and you've never worked a herd in your life."

"Me, I work for me." Robertson gurgled as Slocum squeezed tighter.

"How much is he paying you?"

"Fifty dollars. This ain't worth no fifty dollars. He said you'd sell right off. Kelso never said you'd try to kill me!"

Slocum dropped the man. Robertson fell to the floor, gasping for breath. He wasn't surprised that Robertson had named the real culprit behind the clumsy attempt to purchase the ranch.

"Where'd Kelso get money to buy the place?"

"I don't know. I don't know!" Robertson cowered as Slocum advanced on. "He paid me twenty and said I'd get the rest when you sold. That's all I know!"

"Get off my land. If I see you again, that twenty riding in your pocket ought to be enough for a decent pine coffin."

Roop Robertson scuttled away like a spider, got to his feet, slipped, and then found traction. He raced out the door and less than a minute later, Slocum heard a horse galloping away. A deep breath settled him a mite. He made sure his six-gun slid easily from his holster, then went hunting for Colorado Pete Kelso.

He found him in the bunkhouse, lounging back and swilling from a pint of whiskey.

"I just ran him off," Slocum said. He watched Kelso closely to be sure the man didn't have a pistol hidden under a blanket near his hand. If Kelso so much as twitched, Slocum was going to gun him down. He had reached the end of his rope with his top hand.

"Figured you had from the way Robertson run off like a scalded dog," Kelso said. Slocum was glad the man didn't feign ignorance and irritate him further.

"On your feet."

Kelso downed the rest of his liquor and then tossed the empty bottle at Slocum. He followed the bottle in a rush, fists flying. Slocum dodged the bottle, but could not avoid a heavy fist smashing into his upper arm. He staggered back, trying to get his balance. Kelso kept coming as he pressed his advantage. Slocum caught another punch on his cheek that snapped his head around.

By now cowboys from all around came to see what caused the ruckus.

Slocum put his head down, took a couple more punches to his shoulders, and then charged like an angry bull. He slammed his shoulder into Kelso's belly and lifted the man off the floor. Colorado Pete continued to hammer at his back, but Slocum was beyond feeling the slight damage. He spun Kelso around and heaved him outside. Kelso sprawled in the dirt in front of the bunkhouse.

"Don't," Slocum said, when he saw how Kelso was reaching under his coat. "If you pull a gun, you're dead."

Ryan and Jenks nudged each other, then came over. As Ryan held Kelso down, his partner pulled Kelso's six-gun out and tossed it away.

"So you and your gang gonna murder me?" Kelso glared at Slocum.

Slocum unbuckled his gun belt and handed it to Ryan. A crooked grin came to Kelso's lips. He got to his feet and squared off. This was the last decent expression he would ever have. Slocum unloaded a haymaker that caught Kelso in the center of his face. His nose broke and a spray of bright red blood geysered out. The man staggered and grabbed for his smashed face.

Slocum gauged distances, stepped up, and swung with the full power of arm and body behind the blow. He buried his fist wrist-deep in Kelso's belly.

The man folded like a bad poker hand.

Stepping back, panting harshly, Slocum looked down at his fallen opponent kicking feebly on the ground.

"You're fired," Slocum said. To his surprise, the gathered cowboys all cheered. He looked at Ryan and saw a wide grin on the young man's face. Jenks clapped him on the shoulder, and others crowded in to shake his hand. Slocum had to pull back because he thought he might have cracked a bone or two in his hand with the punch to Kelso's face.

"That sidewinder deserved it," Ryan said. "I was thinkin' on leavin' the Bar-S if I had to put up with him much longer."

"You're the new top hand," Slocum said. "I need a ramrod for the drive to the railhead. You up for it?" He looked at Jenks. If he had thought Ryan's smile was big, it was nothing compared to his partner's.

Slocum bent down and grabbed a handful of shirtfront and pulled Kelso to a sitting position. He knelt and shoved his face close. The smell of blood made his own nostrils flare and his heart beat a little faster again.

"You can keep the horse," Slocum said. "Everything else will be divvied up among the men."

Kelso made some inarticulate sound. Slocum shook him until the man's eyes cleared, and he stared straight at him.

"You and the rustler with the green hat were in cahoots. I don't know if you were part of that gang or if you just happened to tell them where to find Bar-S cattle. It doesn't matter. They're locked up, and maybe you ought to be. There's no proof, but I reckon you've been selling Bar-S cattle to the rustlers. Is that where Robertson's money to buy the Bar-S came from? My own cattle?"

"I'll kill you, Slocum. I'll kill you!" Kelso's threat came amid a new shower of blood as he tried to exhale through his nose.

"Don't make me shoot you, Kelso. I will. You won't be the first—or the last." The coldness of Slocum's words and the steely green eyes fixed on Kelso made the former top hand look away.

"My gear. I want my gear."

"Fetch his saddle, Ryan. Get his horse ready."

"No, no, my gear in the bunkhouse!"

Slocum stood and dragged Kelso to his feet. With a strong shove he got the man walking toward the corral.

"You can't steal my gear," Kelso cried.

"Were you in cahoots with George Gilley, too? Seems rustling dropped off when I ran him out of Colorado, then started again a few weeks later about the time the green-hat gang showed up. You responsible for more than twenty head of Bar-S cattle being stolen?"

"You haven't seen the last of me, Slocum."

"I doubt that. A man like you'd try to shoot me in the back."

"All ready to go, Mr. Slocum," called Ryan. He led Kelso's horse from the corral.

"One minute," Slocum said. "That's all the time you got to make yourself scarce."

Kelso had taken off his bandanna and used it to stanch the flow of blood from his nose. He clumsily mounted and rode away, muttering to himself as he galloped off.

"He's a mean cuss, Mr. Slocum," said Ryan. "You better watch yourself real close. Me and Jenks and the rest'll do what we can."

"I think we've seen the end of rustling," Slocum said, watching the dust cloud settle. Kelso was gone, but he had ridden in the direction of Heavenly. That meant he wasn't likely to go too far. He would belly up to a bar, get himself roaring drunk, and find some Dutch courage in bad whiskey.

Slocum knew he would have to finish the fight started in the bunkhouse sooner or later.

"You reckon he was responsible fer it all?" asked Jenks.

"He probably told the rustlers where to take our beeves so they wouldn't get caught. What we've got will probably fetch a decent price. That means all the more for you boys to share," Slocum said.

A new cheer went up from the cowboys.

He looked at them and said, "I'm not paying you to lolly-gag. Get to work. Get them to work, Ryan."

"Yes, *sir.*"

Slocum waited for his cowboys to disperse and get to their chores. It took a lot of work to keep a ranch in good shape. Without Colorado Pete Kelso, the work would be done a lot quicker.

He walked back to the ranch house and promised himself a long, hot bath to get rid of all the aches. After all he had done in the past couple days, he deserved it.

16

"How many?" Slocum stared in disbelief at Ryan. The young cowboy's grin was huge.

"O'er a thousand, Mr. Slocum. We rounded up o'er a thousand head of cattle, all with the Bar-S brand on their rumps."

Slocum let out a long, low whistle of disbelief. He had worked on Wimmer's ledger, but could not make head nor tail of it. The man had kept meticulous records, but they were all in some code only he could decipher. Or maybe Slocum simply didn't have the book learning needed to figure out the full extent of the Bar-S holdings.

"You're not out rustling cattle to add to the count, are you?"

Ryan laughed and shook his head. "No, sir. That there's the best count we can make. The Bar-S covers a lot of country. Took me and Jenks and the boys a whale of a long time to scout it all. Without any more rustlin' goin' on, why, we have quite a herd."

"Quite a herd," Slocum repeated softly. He was richer than he had ever considered. Louder, he said, "Half of all the profit will be divvied up between you and the rest."

"Half? That'd make us all rich," Ryan said. "Leastways, it'd make us a damn sight richer 'n we are now."

"You all deserve it, sticking with me the way you did."

"Nothing to it. You're a good boss, Mr. Slocum. It's gonna be our pleasure to work fer you as long as you'll have us. And if you keep payin' bonuses like that, you might need a stick to pry us loose. We'll hang on tighter 'n a blood leech in a Louisiana bayou."

Slocum looked across the broad grassy stretch of the high meadow where most of the Bar-S cattle grazed. He imagined three or four other expanses equaling this. There had to be that many if he had a herd so large.

"We ain't seen him either," Ryan said.

"Kelso? Heard tell he was making trouble in town, but when I went in last week, he was gone."

"He's like steppin' in cow shit. No matter how you scrape, there's always some stink left behind. He's not gone too far, mark my words."

"Get the herd bedded down for the night," Slocum said. "We need a decent map to find a trail to the railhead at Montrose that won't work off all the meat on their bones."

"I went on the drive last year," Ryan said. "I think I remember the trail purty good."

"We'll talk it over at chuck," Slocum said. "Are there still strays to the west of here?"

"Saw a few. Not more than ten or so."

"You keep the herd all quiet. I'll see if I can't find those strays." Slocum climbed into the saddle and rode west, the sun bright in his face. The past couple weeks had been close to perfect for him. The rustlers were gone, Kelso had disappeared, and even the fuss about Murphy murdering Jackson Wimmer had quieted down, though Slocum still felt the undercurrent in Heavenly when he went in for supplies at Gutherie's store and to take a nip or two of Gutherie's booze. Life was as good as it had been in a passel of years. The only thing Slocum missed was seeing Suzanne Underwood, and he reckoned she was spending her time out at Murphy's Circle M.

Slocum rode down into a ravine, then followed it around to come out near a clump of trees where a spring burbled up. He smelled the sulfur in the air and cursed. He didn't want his cows drinking from a hot spring. Too much mineral made them sickly. He had seen some cattle drinking from sulfurous ponds, then the cows just upped and died. Not that he was getting greedy, wanting as many cows as possible to be driven into the stockyards, but he didn't like seeing any animal sicken and die.

His nose wrinkled as he neared the spring. The rocks were stained bright yellow from the sulfur and more than one small, picked-clean carcass near the edge of the pond told him how dangerous drinking this water was. A larger animal might not die, but it wasn't healthy no matter the size. He had heard tell that on the other side of the mountains, over in Manitou Springs, people from back East paid huge sums of money to bathe in sulfur water. Taking the waters was supposed to cure what ailed them, from arthritis to ague and tuberculosis, but they weren't drinking the water.

A lowing from farther west caused him to turn his horse's face in that direction and away from the sulfur spring. He was glad that the cattle had either not found the sulfur spring or had left it behind. Slocum put his spurs to his mare's flanks and got the dun moving at a trot.

He saw a dozen head of cattle grazing peaceably in a narrow draw not a quarter mile ahead. As he rode, Slocum worked through numbers in his head. He could sell off a fair number of cattle, make a profit, and still have enough head left to get a good start on the next year's herd. The Bar-S was going to be successful for a long, long time at this rate.

"Bar-S," he said to himself as he guided his horse down into the narrow channel leading toward his strays. "Where'd the name come from?"

Jackson Wimmer was the kind of man who would have named the ranch after himself. The Bar-W maybe, or the J-Bar-W. Slocum decided this was just one more thing about Wimmer and his legacy that would never come to light. He had never asked, but Wimmer might have bought the ranch from an earlier owner. If so, changing the brand might have been more trouble than it was worth, though after a couple seasons, running a pair of brands would no longer be necessary.

"Come on, you mangy cows," Slocum shouted. He unfastened his rope and played out a ten-foot length. Whirling the end around his head made a whistling sound that got the attention of the beeves. They looked up from their afternoon meal with dull brown eyes.

Then all hell broke loose. Slocum was forming them into a smaller herd to get moving when a half dozen more cattle came thundering down the draw from higher up on the hillside.

The frightened run of the other cattle spooked the ones Slocum was working. He looked from side to side, and knew he had no room to get out of the way of the stampeding cattle. That left only one thing to do. He swung about and raked his spurs along the dun's sides, leaving bloody streaks. The frightened horse lit out like its tail was on fire. Slocum hunkered down, head next to the straining horse's neck.

"Come on, run, run!"

The horse's hooves pounded hard on the ground, but Slocum felt new vibration. Thirty head of cattle came closer and closer behind. He heard them and smelled them and felt their panic. The fear transmitted itself to his horse and caused it to balk.

"Not now, run, run, run, damn you, run!"

Slocum did not quite regain control of the horse, but did get it galloping along. He was content to give the horse its head—for the moment. It remained in the narrow channel cut by years of heavy spring runoff from higher elevations, but Slocum realized he had to get out fast when his horse began to flag. With every step, the animal weakened. Its terror grew and it started to toss its head about.

Slocum chanced a look over his shoulder. The cattle were so close he could almost feel their hot breaths. He did see wide bovine eyes completely ringed by white. Their fright was not lessening and neither was their headlong stampede.

Swinging his weight and using his right knee to press into the horse's flank turned it enough for it to stumble up a slope. The dun scrambled onto the lip of the draw and stumbled a few more paces. Slocum drew rein and halted its panicky run. The horse's flanks heaved as its mighty lungs sucked in air. Slocum patted the horse's neck and calmed it the best he could.

The stampeding cattle had raced on down the ravine, and had come to a spot where the high walls turned lower, allowing the cattle to spread out. As they did so, their panic eased.

"That was a close shave," Slocum said. He pushed his hat back and mopped at his forehead with his bandanna. He remained where he was, not bothering to herd the cattle. They headed in the right direction. Ryan or another of his hands would spot the beeves and get them into the main herd.

Slocum wanted to do a bit of exploring. It took some doing, but he got his horse back down into the draw and started uphill again. When he reached the spot where he had found the cattle grazing, he studied the ground. It had been so badly cut up by the cattle's hooves he could make out nothing more than that the cattle had eaten all the grass there. He rode slowly farther up the draw, and found where the other cattle had come charging down to spook the cattle he had first found.

He stepped down and examined the ground more carefully. His finger traced around a deep hoofprint in the soft earth. He could still make out where the horseshoe had been nailed on. Slocum looked around, but whoever had ridden here was long gone.

Refusing to simply ignore his brush with being trampled, he prowled about restlessly, getting the picture of what had happened. The cattle in the draw were a lure for him. A lone rider had stampeded another dozen cattle and caused the tide of frightened beef that had almost overwhelmed him. The conclusion was inescapable. Someone had tried to kill him.

"Who might that be?" Slocum asked himself. He had a score to settle with Colorado Pete Kelso because he couldn't think of anyone else inclined to do such a thing. As he started to mount, something colorful fluttering nearby caught his eye. Pulling his foot back out of the stirrup, he went to the low thorn bush and tugged the bandanna free from the nettles.

Holding it up to the light to see it better, Slocum turned it over and over. He recognized the distinctive orange kerchief as the one Seamus Murphy had worn when the marshal had clapped him into jail. Slocum started to cry out about the stupidity of the Irish rancher. Trying to kill the only man who had tried to get him free of the law seemed monumentally stupid. Then Slocum calmed a mite.

It *was* stupid. There was no reason for even a hothead like Seamus Murphy to kill Slocum. Even if he carried a grudge, it was hardly the biggest or worst. Slocum could see Murphy gunning down the marshal or taking on half the town for what they said about him, but there was no point in putting Slocum at the head of the list.

Unless . . .

The uneasy crawling in his gut warned Slocum that he might have trespassed, on property Murphy considered his own. Had Suzanne Underwood let slip that she and Slocum had spent time together? That would set off most any man, being cuckolded. Worse, Slocum could see Suzanne holding it over Murphy, telling him she was going off with the richest man in Middle Park. That would be a double sting to a touchy man's pride.

Slocum tucked the bandanna into his coat pocket, and set out to track the man responsible for driving the cattle down into the draw and causing the stampede. At first, the trail was confused by the cattle trampling the dirt. He cast out a bit farther and found a single set of fresh hoofprints going away from the draw.

Buoyed by the sight of such distinct tracks, Slocum rode faster. Now and then he lifted his gaze to the horizon to be sure he wasn't riding into an ambush, but from the way the rider had whipped his horse to a gallop, Slocum knew he was following a man who wanted nothing more than to get the hell away from the scene of his crime.

His would-be crime. Slocum touched the butt of the pistol slung at his left hip, then rode faster. It was almost dusk when he lost the trail. The rider had gone across a broad stretch of rock. In daylight, Slocum might have found bright scratches where steel horseshoes had nicked the rock, but in the twilight, such a pursuit was impossible.

Stretching, he looked around. It was quite a ride, but he could get over a ridge of mountains and drop down on the far side—onto Seamus Murphy's land. Slocum knew he should have told Ryan or another of his cowboys where he was headed, but he felt an itch to settle scores.

He crested the ridge and worked down a trail on the far side, and eventually came to the narrow road leading to Murphy's cabin. The stretch of road ahead had been nothing but misery for Slocum, but he rode on. This time he didn't get his horse shot out from under him. He halted and stared at the cabin when he came to the clearing. A wispy curl of wood smoke rose from the chimney, but Slocum knew better than to assume Murphy was inside. His caution paid off when he heard grunting and sloshing.

Murphy made his way from the spring some distance away, lugging two fully filled buckets. In the darkness, Murphy did not see him. Slocum dismounted and walked closer. He made certain the leather keeper had been slipped away from the hammer of his Colt Navy. If the need arose, he could slap leather and get his six-shooter blazing in the wink of an eye.

The Irishman whistled between his teeth as he dumped both buckets of water into a barrel beside the front door. He started back for the spring when Slocum called out his name. Murphy froze.

"Slocum?"

"I want a word with you. Turn around real slow and keep both those buckets in your hands. Go for a gun and you're a dead man."

"Go on, cut me down. You might as well shoot me in the back. It's what the rest of you people want to do."

"Who's that?"

"Anyone in Heavenly. Everyone. They keep hopin' I won't be able to pay the mortgage on the ranch so they can run me out. They won't do it! I'm not givin' up!"

"Heard tell that you were behind in payment to the bank, but you haven't been foreclosed on yet."

"They're thinkin' on it."

"You've got a chip on your shoulder."

"And you've got the drop on me. Either shoot me in the back or get off my property."

Slocum dropped the reins and walked around to where Murphy could see that he had yet to draw his six-shooter.

"You been over on my land today?"

"That's none of your business."

"I'm making it mine," Slocum said. He pulled the orange bandanna from his pocket. "This yours?"

"Looks like the one I lost. Don't see many that color, so, yeah, reckon it's mine."

"Where'd you lose it? I saw you wearing it when you were locked up."

"For a trumped-up rustling charge!"

"Where did you lose it?"

Murphy dropped his water buckets. He thrust out his chin truculently, as if daring Slocum to take a swing at him. The way Slocum felt at the moment, it wouldn't be his fist smashing into the young man's face. A single bullet would serve his purposes better. But he held back.

"Where did you lose it? I'm not going to ask again."

"I don't know. I had it when Zamora let me out of jail. I got back here and took it off, thinking to wash it."

Slocum ran his fingers over the grimy cloth. It hadn't been washed in a month of Sundays.

"Did you?"

"I must have dropped it. I took a bath and washed my clothes. But I couldn't find it." He shrugged. "Thought the wind had taken it. I'd just piled my clothes out front while I was rootin' around inside the house huntin' for other things to wash."

"What else?"

"Bedsheets. That was it."

Slocum stepped closer. Murphy's bravado cracked, and he took an involuntary step back. His eyes went wide when Slocum took a deep sniff.

"Show me your bed."

"I ain't—"

"Show me."

"All right, Slocum. You're not going to—"

Slocum shoved him into the cabin and went to the narrow bed. All he had to do was touch the sheet to know Murphy had been telling the truth. It had been washed recently.

"You been here all day?"

"I've been here since I got out of jail, if it's any concern of yours."

Slocum pulled the orange bandanna from his coat pocket and tossed it to Murphy.

"Needs cleaning."

Slocum left the rancher with his mouth gaping and a hundred unasked questions on his lips. He mounted his dun mare and rode away, thinking hard. Somebody had gone to a bit of trouble to frame Murphy. If Slocum had been killed in the stampede, his ranch hands would have found the bandanna and probably recognized it. Whether they went to the marshal or simply strung up Murphy wouldn't much matter. Both Murphy and Slocum would be dead.

Something made Slocum even more curious, though. If he had not asked some questions, he might have gunned down Murphy. Was that good enough for whoever had stampeded the cattle? Killing Murphy looked to be the result, no matter what happened to Slocum.

That was more than curious. It was downright diabolical.

17

"There might be a couple strays still in the high pasture, Mr. Slocum, but fetchin' 'em in for the drive's not gonna matter one whit." Ryan took off his dusty Stetson and banged it against his thigh. A cloud of brown trail dust billowed up. He slapped it once more and then settled the hat squarely on his head, the brim touching the tops of both ears.

"We'll need some supplies from town," Slocum said, "for the drive. Otherwise, we're ready."

"Counted close to eleven hunnerd cattle," Ryan said. He looked sheepish and said, "Jenks counted 'em. I'm not too good at cipherin'."

"Have him teach you. I don't want a top hand who can't count higher than the total of his fingers and toes."

"That'd be eighteen," Ryan said. Seeing Slocum's reaction, he added, "Froze two toes off last winter."

"Least you know how many you've got," Slocum said, laughing. He was pleased with the roundup. He had cattle he had not found listed in Jackson Wimmer's ledger—and all carried the Bar-S brand. They were his cattle to do with as he saw fit.

That posed something of a problem for him. He could sell all the cattle and make a few extra dollars, or leave some in the pastureland for breeding next year's herd. If he did that, it meant he intended to stay and become a full-time rancher.

"You thinkin' hard on something, Mr. Slocum? I found that there map of the trail to Montrose. I kin read maps a whole lot better 'n I do books. This will be a trail I've ridden before."

"Last year," Slocum said, his mind wandering. How many cattle to keep back? It would have to be the prize heifers, some calves, and maybe a pair of bulls.

"Who you want to send into town for the supplies?"

Slocum shook himself out of his reverie. It took a couple seconds to remember what had gone on.

"Who deserves a break from riding herd?"

"Reckon we all do. But it wouldn't be a good thing to let ever' one of us go into town. Those saloons are a big attraction when you have a couple dimes in your pocket."

"I'd get back a dozen drunk cowboys, is that it?"

"You'd have to bail us all out of Marshal Zamora's lockup. I don't cotton much to bein' the only sober one crammed into one of them cells with drunks," Ryan said. "But if any of the boys got into a row, I'd hafta go to his aid."

Slocum laughed again. It felt good not to be tense and on guard all the time. It felt good to be a rancher and to be looking at a powerful lot of money from a decent herd.

Slocum heard himself saying, "Send a couple boys into town for the supplies. You and Jenks get back to the herd and cut out three hundred of the best to use as breeding stock for next season."

"Yes, *sir*," Ryan said. He let out a whoop and tossed his hat high into the air.

"Why so excited?"

"I just won a twenty-dollar bet with Jenks. He said you wasn't stickin' 'round next year. Yippee!" Ryan raced off to spread the news. Slocum settled back on the front porch of the ranch house—his ranch house. He looked across the yard to the bunkhouse and the barn and the corral filled with horses. All his. It was quite a responsibility, but that part had never gnawed away much at Slocum. His entire life had been filled with doing what was right. This seemed right, even if it meant giving up his wandering to find what lay just beyond the horizon.

"The Bar-S is what lay at the end of the trail," Slocum said. He rocked back in a chair and listened to the flies buzzing, the horses moving about in the corral, and all the other comforting sounds of a ranch.

Ryan and Jenks rode to the high pasture to select the stock for next year. Slocum would check, but doubted either man would go far wrong in his choices. A few minutes after that, the buckboard with three other men rattled off down the road toward Heavenly, intent on fetching supplies for the trail drive. The smaller sounds Slocum had heard before now became the only ones reaching him.

Until he heard something moving inside his house. Without hurrying, he reached across his belly and laid his hand on the ebony handle of his six-gun. He turned his head a little to get a better look at the front door. It had blown open in the weak breeze stirring around. Through the opening he caught a quick reflection in a mirror and an indistinct body moving across the far window, now lit with noonday sun.

Slocum rocked forward and got to his feet. He slid his six-shooter from its holster and went to the door. Using the toe of his boot, he pushed it wide open and lifted the muzzle to sight in on . . . Suzanne Underwood.

She jumped when she saw him in the door, his gun pointed at her. A hand fluttered to her throat and she let out a tiny gasp.

"Oh, John, you scared me. It seems like you're always pointing that thing at me."

He dropped his pistol back into his holster, went inside, and kicked the door shut with his heel. Looking at the woman was about as delicious as sitting on the porch and realizing everything he saw was his personal property. Suzanne had on a new floral print dress made of thinner fabric than the white one he had seen her wearing that first time long ago in Heavenly. The day was warm and she had sweat a mite. The cloth plastered itself to her chest and made her breasts look as if they had been upholstered. The nipples were visible and so inviting, it was hard for Slocum to take his eyes off them.

"You came in the back way."

"I didn't want your men to see me."

"If you drove your buggy, they saw it when they left for town."

"I . . . sold it. All I have now is a horse to ride." She rubbed her backside. "It's been a while, and I'm not used to long miles yet."

She saw how he stared at her as she ran her hands over her curvy hindquarters, and smiled.

"Am I amusing you?"

"Can't say that," he admitted. "More like giving me quite a show."

"A show? Whatever can you mean?" Her hands left her pert rump and dropped to her sides. Fingers curling, she grabbed double handfuls of cloth and began raising her skirt off the floor. Her high-button shoes and trim ankles appeared. But she did not stop as she lifted more and gave him a look of bare calf.

"If you give me much more of a show, I'm not certain where I should sit to watch it."

"Sit anywhere you like, but I don't want you only watching," Suzanne said. Her tongue slipped between her ruby lips and made a slow circuit. "No, John, I don't want you just watching. I want you to be *participating*."

She moved slowly toward him, lifting her skirt even higher so he could see bare legs. When she was about arm's length away, she widened her stance and kept pulling up her skirt with a soft rustle. Slocum hardly noticed the sound. He was too intent on her bare skin and that she wasn't wearing any underwear.

"I knew I'd see pretty vistas when I came to Colorado," Slocum said. He unfastened his gun belt and laid it on the desk. Then he reached out and ran his fingers over the sleek curves of her breasts. She had been sweating more than he thought. His fingers turned slick. He caught one nipple through the cloth and twisted it slightly. Suzanne closed her eyes and moaned softly.

"I want more, John," she said. "I want only what *you* can give me."

She gasped when he began giving both breasts the same treatment. Then he slid his fingers under the cloth and peeled it slowly off her skin. Unbuttoning her blouse took a little doing, but feeling her heat and silken skin made it worthwhile. He tossed her blouse to the floor, leaving her naked to the waist.

"How do you want me?"

In answer, Slocum put his hands around her slender waist and lifted. She let out a cry of surprise as her feet left the floor. Then she landed hard on the edge of the desk. She put her hands on her breasts and began massaging them.

"What now?"

Slocum ran his hands up her calves and slid her skirt away, just as he had stripped her of her blouse. When her skirt bunched around her waist, she looked more naked than dressed. He dropped to his knees and let her dangle her legs over his shoulders. This brought his face in close so he could lick and kiss her nether lips.

She leaned back, supporting herself on her elbows. Of their own volition, her knees rose until she placed her feet on the edge of the desk. Her knees parted, letting him have full access to her most intimate region.

Slocum drove his tongue forward and tasted the salty tang of an aroused woman. Using his tongue, he dipped and dived, sucked and slid it all around, until she trembled like she was seized with a fever.

"More, John. This is so good, but I want more. I want *you*."

He was in no hurry. He continued to kiss across the thick dark bush and moved upward slowly to her belly. His tongue repeated with her navel what it had done lower. He felt her stomach quiver at his damp touch. Then he skipped over the thick wad of skirt and found the deep canyon between her breasts.

"Oh, don't stop, John. I want this. Oh, how I want this!"

She laced her fingers behind his head to hold him down at her breasts. He spiraled up one snowy mound, toyed with the hard pink nipple he found, then skied down into the deep valley to repeat his action on the other side. When he caught this nipple between his lips, he sucked hard and drew it across his teeth. She arched her back and then flopped weakly onto the desk.

"More," she gasped out. "More, more."

Her legs were still draped over his shoulders. He reached up and drew her closer. His crotch pressed into hers.

"Free you, get you out." She reached around and hurriedly unbuttoned him. He snapped free of his cloth prison—and sank immediately into her heated center.

Legs over his shoulders, she was bent double. As he thrust forward, he pressed her upper thighs down into her breasts. She recoiled, pushing him back. He slid from her.

"No, not that. No!"

He slid back into her heated tightness. The moisture he had tasted now made his erection slick. He moved faster. The friction built until the carnal heat erupted like prairie fire. It consumed him and then it consumed her. Slocum was not sure of anything but the intense sensations that ripped through him and then left him panting for breath.

He backed away, letting her legs drop to either side of his hips. Suzanne wore a smile of pure delight. Her eyes flickered open and the smile grew even more.

"So nice, John. You know exactly what I need."

"Maybe sometime we can do this in a bed. I've got a big one in the bedroom." The instant the words left his lips, he saw the change in her. She looked away and whatever resid-ual bliss there had been evaporated.

"Yes, that would be nice," she said, sitting up. She still did not look him in the eye as she moved off the desk and tried to smooth her skirt down over her legs. She was still bare to the waist. When he handed her the discarded blouse, she took it, still avoiding his direct gaze.

He watched her complete dressing with a mixture of loss and curiosity. If he had ever entertained any notion of settling down with Suzanne, it was gone now. But why? It wasn't anything he had done, but he couldn't see why mentioning making love in a bed would turn her so cold so quickly.

Slocum strapped his six-shooter on and waited until Suzanne completed her toilet.

"You came by for something. What was it?"

"Why, I thought we just did it," she said, but there was no passion in her words. It was as if she read from a prepared text.

"That was icing on the cake. What's the cake?"

"Oh, John, you can be so vexing. Why must you always get down to business so fast? You're just like—" Suzanne cut off her sentence abruptly. He waited for her to finish. He wanted to know who he was like, but she changed her tack. "I need a favor."

"Money?"

"No!" Her sharp retort put roses into her cheeks and fire into her eyes again. Then she took a deep breath. Somehow, the sight of those magnificent breasts rising and falling didn't move him the way it once had. "I want a favor from you."

"Seamus Murphy?"

Anger flared for a moment, then she softened. "What you must think of me," she said. "Yes. Seamus Murphy. Nobody in Heavenly likes him."

"From what he says, they all want to string him up."

"They think he killed Jackson Wimmer. He'd never do that."

"Any crime seems to have his name written on it," Slocum said, thinking of how Marshal Zamora had been so eager to brand him a rustler. The notion that Murphy might have tried to kill him with the stampede also rose in Slocum's mind, but he was good at reading men. He had made money playing poker for years and knew bluffs from the truth—most of the time. While Murphy might have gulled him, Slocum thought the young rancher was telling the truth about losing the orange bandanna. That meant someone was trying to frame him.

"He works hard on his ranch," she said. "He knows what he's doing. It's just that he has never gotten a chance to prosper."

"The bank is threatening to foreclose," Slocum said. "That's why I thought you wanted to ask me for money."

"To give to Seamus?" Suzanne shook her head. "He's too proud to accept a gift. Or even a loan. His pa had reason to hate bankers, and it rubbed off on Seamus."

"What's your part in this?"

"I . . . after what we did, it seems wrong . . . I—"

"Never mind," Slocum said. He knew that Suzanne Underwood would do whatever she could for Seamus Murphy. Although he had never seen the two of them together when they weren't arguing, it went along with what he knew of Murphy's character. He was as rough as a dried corncob. And Suzanne was smoother than silk.

"He needs your help, John. I'm begging you for it."

"Might be he should pull up stakes and go somewhere else," Slocum said. He waited for her reaction. It didn't take but an instant and he was not disappointed.

"We'd never do a thing like that! Why, this is his home. He's worked hard to prove that ranch. He's not the sort to give up because the going got tough."

Slocum nodded slowly. This was what he had hoped to hear—and matched what he had seen in Seamus Murphy. Too often the West provided enough space for a man to keep moving to run away from his problems. They always caught up, but the open horizons let him keep going. That Murphy was willing to dig in his heels and fight for his ranch and a place in the community set well with Slocum.

"What do you want me to do that I haven't already? I got him out of jail after he was arrested for rustling, and you said you don't want money to pay off the bank."

"The murder charge against him," Suzanne said. She looked as if she had bitten into a persimmon. "You know he didn't kill Wimmer, but someone did. If you can catch his killer, that will clear Seamus."

"It doesn't seem that Marshal Zamora is going to work too hard to find anyone other than Murphy," Slocum said. He looked up at the hole in the ceiling. Where had that come from? His eyes drifted to the bare spot on the wall where a picture had hung. Somehow, those went together, but he had no idea why.

"Nobody in town will believe Seamus didn't kill Wimmer, but with someone on trial for the crime, that'll go a ways to easing Seamus's mind," she said.

Slocum looked at her sharply. That made no sense. What did Murphy care who killed Wimmer and why would finding the real murderer ease his mind?

"Kelso," he said. As if the pot had finally come to a boil and that name rose to the churning surface, he knew.

"The son of a bitch," Suzanne said. "He wouldn't leave me alone. He loved me, he said. I'd sooner go to bed with a diamondback rattler."

"He was sweet on you, and you're sweet on Murphy. Kelso wanted to frame Murphy for whatever he could. He was the one who got the drop on Murphy and accused him of rustling." Slocum's mind raced. It had been a while since he'd laid eyes on Kelso. There was no telling where he had ended up.

It might well have been out in the west pasture so he could stampede part of the herd in Slocum's direction.

"How'd Kelso get Murphy's bandanna?"

"What?" Suzanne's eyes went wide in surprise. "I didn't know that he had it."

Slocum quickly explained what had happened to him.

"Seamus would never do a thing like that. If he wanted to kill a man, he'd walk right up to him and have it out."

"I believe you're right. His temper tells me he's not the sneaky kind."

"If that's a compliment, thank you," Suzanne said. She looked at him skeptically.

"Kelso left his gear in the bunkhouse. I want to see what's there."

They went to the empty bunkhouse. It took Slocum a few minutes of poking around to find the box where Ryan had shoved it. Suzanne sat on a bunk as Slocum knelt and began rummaging through what was mostly junk.

"There, John, that's Seamus's spare spoon. It's got his brand etched into it. He lost it after I—" Suzanne looked hard at Slocum, then summoned her courage. "He couldn't it find after I spent the night with him for the first time."

"You used the spoon?"

"I don't understand what that has to do with anything."

"If Kelso was following you and saw, he might have stolen the spoon to have something of yours. Something you used."

"He could have stolen Seamus's six-shooter to frame him! And his bandanna! There's no telling what else he might have taken."

"All of it to remind him of you and to get back at Murphy. If he got Murphy convicted, he'd be free to court you."

"Never in a million years!"

"When a man's crazy in love, things like that don't matter," Slocum said. "I suspect Kelso is both crazy in love and just plain loco."

"Do you think he murdered Wimmer?"

Again Slocum heard the bitterness in her voice, but knew better than to try to find its source.

"He had reason enough to do it and then frame Murphy. If Murphy and I hadn't been in town together, it might have worked."

"Prove it, John, please. Prove it." Suzanne chewed her lower lip, then stood and went to the bunkhouse door. She turned and started to say something, thought better of it, and rushed out.

Slocum kept pawing through the box and found a framed picture buried at the bottom. He pulled it out. It was about the right size to have been taken off the wall in Wimmer's office. Holding it up, he looked at the faded photograph of a much younger Jackson Wimmer and a girl who could not have been older than five or six.

He pushed the box back where Ryan had stored it, but he took the picture to the ranch house and hung it where it had once been proudly displayed by a crusty old curmudgeon.

The frame neatly covered the unfaded area on the wall. This was the picture that had been removed by Kelso, probably when he had killed Jackson Wimmer. Now all Slocum had to do was prove it.

18

"Shore thing, Mr. Slocum. We got this here herd ready to move," Ryan said. "Don't go worryin' your head over it none."

"You're doing good," Slocum said. The cattle filled the pasture. As far as the eye could see, brown and white and black movement told of the huge herd ready to drive to market. Ryan had selected well for the start of next year's herd also. Slocum felt safe in letting the young man keep order in camp until he got back.

"You be gone long?" Ryan asked.

"Don't think so," Slocum said. He looked up the draw where he had almost been killed by the stampede. He had been distracted before by Murphy's kerchief. Although it had been a while, he thought he could find the trail of the man who had tried to kill him—Colorado Pete Kelso.

He and Colorado Pete had some serious talking to do, and it wasn't just about the stampede.

"We got a week, maybe two before the weather changes on us," said Ryan. "This high up in the mountains, the weather's always a bitch. Can't predict from one day to the next."

"I won't be more than a day. If I am, take the cattle on into Montrose and wait for me there."

"I'd have to feed them in Montrose. Feedlot prices are mighty steep, and I can't negotiate the price for you. You're the owner of the Bar-S, after all."

"I'll be back," Slocum said, slapping Ryan on the shoulder. He appreciated the way his new top hand worried about the details. Swinging into the saddle, Slocum turned toward the west and headed out. It took less than an hour to find the draw, and two hours to convince himself he had found a faint trail leading not to Seamus Murphy's ranch but farther westward.

The notion that he might be following a ghost trail worried him a little. Then he saw how the trail circled around and headed for a pass that would put him onto the road leading into Heavenly. At this point, Slocum stopped studying the ground and started riding harder. His dun pony protested a mite, but kept him heading toward his target. Heavenly was as likely a place for Kelso to go as anywhere else since Slocum doubted he would stray far from Suzanne Underwood. The man was obsessed with her.

As he reached the road and turned toward town, Slocum wondered how far that obsession would take Kelso. Kidnap? Murder? Either was likely for a back-shooting son of a bitch like Pete Kelso. He had tried to get Murphy hanged rather than facing his rival for Suzanne's affection man-to-man. Slocum turned grim. Kelso would do anything to get the woman. Anything.

Thinking about Suzanne caused a knot to form in Slocum's belly. He was taken with her, but she was devoted to Seamus Murphy and would do anything for him that she could. Slocum saw the two of them as standing against the townspeople of Heavenly, but what drew them together was more than that. If he disengaged his emotions enough, he could see that Seamus and Suzanne were quite a pair.

"Lucky bastard," Slocum said, a rueful smile on his lips. His horse turned its head and looked up at him quizzically. A quick pat reassured the mare that all was well.

All he had to do was track down Kelso and ask a few simple questions. The answers would put Colorado Pete in jail for a long time, if they didn't get him a noose.

As Slocum rode into Heavenly, he passed the courthouse. A flash of movement caught out of the corner of his eye made him draw rein and look more carefully at low bushes under a window. The movement there did not come from a vagrant breeze. Slocum turned his pony's face toward the side of the courthouse, and was quick enough to duck when a man popped up like a prairie dog and opened fire on him.

Slocum struggled to get his horse under control. By the time he did, the gunman was gone—and a new danger presented itself. The bushes flared high with a greasy smoke and orange flame that licked at the side of the building.

"Fire!" Slocum shouted. "Ring the alarm. Fire!"

Seconds later came the clanging of the fire bell from the far side of town. Fire was more to be feared than anything else. It struck fast and could consume every building in Heavenly within minutes. Most of the structures had been built leaning against each other with no thought to safety. Materials were dried and flammable, and if the fire spread to either of the saloons, all that could be done was evacuate everyone to a safe distance and watch the town burn.

Horses neighed loudly and a smaller bell rang furiously. Slocum saw a pumper truck careening down the middle of the main street, the driver half dressed and the team almost out of control.

"Where's the fire? Where's the danged fire?"

"Courthouse," Slocum shouted. "You got water in that tank?"

"Hell, no. Need to run the hose over to the creek."

Slocum lashed his horse securely to a hitching post and helped the volunteer fireman uncoil the thick canvas hose.

"Where's the stream?"

"Yonder," the fireman said, pointing. "Hurry it up. The whole damn side of the whole damn building's on fire!"

Slocum slung the hose over his shoulder, leaned forward, dug in his toes, and started pulling. The heavy hose snaked out behind him as he sought the creek. A line of vegetation drew him. He couldn't hear the murmur of water as it cascaded over rocks due to the tumult in town now. Worse, the crackling of the fire threatened to drown out even fervent shouts of encouragement.

Slocum gave one last tug and dropped the hose to the bank. He found a deep pool, waded in, and pulled the hose after him.

"Start pumping!" His shout might have been heard, or the fireman could have figured there was no harm beginning the steam pump. The hose bucked about as it drew water. Slocum fought to hold it underwater. His arms ached from the effort, and finally he found a way to wedge the hose between two large rocks and pile others atop it to hold it in the stream. Sloshing, he climbed from the water and ran back to the fire.

Three men held the hose attached to the pump. The man who had driven the pumper rig stood next to the steam engine, cursing, kicking the balky machinery, and sometimes making small adjustments with a big wrench. Whether it was the wrench or the cursing, Slocum didn't know, but the engine kept turning and the pump provided a powerful flow of water.

He watched as the water arched up into the air and crashed down on the side of the two-story courthouse. The whitewashed wall had turned a sooty black and in some places the fire had burned through, but the prompt arrival of the pumper had prevented fiery disaster from destroying the building and the town.

"What happened, Slocum?"

He looked around to see Marshal Zamora. The man stared with wide, frightened eyes at the dwindling fire. Slocum had seen horses with the same look before they turned and galloped back into a burning barn.

"I saw a man in the bushes. The next thing I know, he took a shot at me and the fire started. I didn't get a real good look at him."

"Everyone out of the building?"

Slocum stared at the courthouse. Water continued to extinguish smaller fires that popped up.

"Don't know."

"Better go look." Zamora strode off with forced courage. Slocum reckoned the man was afraid of fires. He couldn't much blame him. He had been in more than one wildfire in his day, and they were nothing to take lightly.

"Damn me," Zamora said, pulling open the front door. A cloud of black smoke billowed out. "This is enough to make me get a decent job."

"I'll go in," Slocum said. He pushed past the marshal and went into the smoke-filled lobby. Four rooms led off the small area. Stairs at the rear went to the second floor where there would be more rooms. Eyes stinging from the acrid smoke, Slocum bent low and saw a pair of boots toward the rear of the lobby.

"Can you get to him, Slocum?"

The lawman squatted down and peered under the layer of thick smoke. He had seen the man, too.

"I'll get him out." As Slocum started to go to the rescue, the man rolled over and he got a good look at his face. "Murphy!"

Calling his name galvanized Seamus Murphy into motion. He rolled back onto his belly and wiggled like a snake to get out the back way. Slocum followed and burst out the back door and collided with Marshal Zamora.

"The son of a bitch lit out 'fore I got around," the lawman said. "I'll have his hide nailed to the barn door for this."

"Why? He was caught in the fire."

"He set the damn fire," shouted Zamora. "There's no other reason for that worthless cayuse to be in the courthouse."

Slocum said nothing as he wiped soot from his face. Zamora shouted to the volunteer firemen putting out the last of the sparks threatening to jump to other roofs. In a few minutes, Zamora came back holding a hat. He shook it at Slocum.

"See? See?"

"You've got a hat that's been burned. So?"

"It's Murphy's hat. I recognize the hatband made from those crazy Irish knots. It was in those bushes where the fire started. He's a firebug as well as a murderer."

"He didn't kill Wimmer, and he didn't set the fire. The man I saw in the bushes had his hat pulled down low when he took off running."

"You keep your nose out of this, Slocum. I don't know why you're stickin' up for that varmint, but you'll swing beside him if you don't watch yourself."

"Don't threaten me, Marshal."

"It's not a threat as long as I'm wearing this badge." Zamora tapped the battered star on his chest. "I have to keep the peace. Killing Wimmer might be somethin' nobody cared much about, but burning down the courthouse goes too far." Marshal Zamora swung around and shouted for volunteer deputies.

Slocum saw that the lawman intended to put a posse onto Murphy's trail, only it looked less like a posse and more like a lynch mob as the angry men gathered. Old hatreds had bubbled up and consumed them, making Murphy's lynching a certainty if they caught him. He stayed at the edge of the mob as Zamora whipped up their passion against Seamus Murphy. Saying a word in defense of the rancher would have gotten him strung up, so Slocum moved away and looked around the bushes where he had seen the man who had set the fire.

The shrubs were burned to bare limbs and provided no evidence. The ground had been turned to mud from the deluge from the pumper truck. Slocum went into the courthouse and poked around. The stench of burned wood choked him, but he kept looking and finally stood where he had seen Murphy.

The door to the county clerk's office stood open. Slocum went in.

On the floor lay a ledger. He stepped over it and looked for some reason Murphy might have come here. This wasn't the land office. If there had been a problem with his land deed, he would not have come here. Hardly noticing, Slocum bent and picked up the ledger and returned it to the counter.

He blinked as he saw Murphy's signature on the bottom line. Slocum closed the book and muttered to himself. Seamus Murphy had come to the courthouse to get a marriage license. Knowing that the evidence of why the rancher was in town would mean nothing to Zamora, and even less to a mob all riled up and ready to stretch Murphy's neck, Slocum knew what had to be done. He had to find the arsonist and make him confess.

Finding Murphy's hat where the fire started told Slocum who had set the fire. Colorado Pete Kelso had tried to frame Murphy before. Several times before, unless Slocum was completely mistaken. Kelso must have taken Murphy's gun and used it to kill Wimmer, then had left the young rancher's bandanna to implicate him in the stampede. Now he'd tried to frame Murphy for the fire, probably not only because Murphy loved Suzanne, but also because the young rancher wanted to marry her.

Kelso had a lot to answer for.

Marshal Zamora had finally gotten the mob mounted and headed out of town in the direction of Murphy's ranch. Slocum hoped Seamus had the good sense not to return to his cabin. He sucked in a breath, wondering what Zamora would do—or allow—if his posse found Suzanne Underwood at the cabin. Hanging a woman was not something even a blood-crazed mob would do lightly, but it was a sorry event that could not be discounted.

This made Slocum all the more eager to find Kelso and force a confession from him. Nothing less would save

Murphy from the hangman's noose or Suzanne from what the posse might do to her.

Slocum fetched his horse and rode out of town following the posse. Tracking Kelso wouldn't be possible, but figuring where the owlhoot might go was easy enough. He wanted the posse to go after Murphy, and the likely place they would find the rancher was on his own property. Slocum remembered a hill looking down into Circle M land that might give a good view of the cabin. Kelso would want to see Murphy's heels kicking in the air because that would complete his revenge for Suzanne choosing the wrong man. In his head, Kelso might even think this would leave Suzanne open to him courting her again.

It suddenly occurred to Slocum how he himself might turn this to his own advantage. Let the marshal string up Murphy, and Suzanne might fall into another man's bed—his. Barely had the idea blossomed in Slocum's head than it withered. He would never do that to get a woman. Though he had not quite come out and promised, he had assured Suzanne that he wouldn't let anything happen to her lover. More than this, any fire that might have blazed between him and the lovely woman was now turned to ashes.

"The man signed the county ledger to get a marriage license," Slocum mused.

He urged his pony into a trot, cut off the road, and struck out across the countryside, finding hilly land fast. The horse struggled to get up the steep slope, but Slocum eventually came to the top of a ridge looking down over Murphy's rangeland. It would be a while before the posse reached Murphy's cabin, giving Slocum time enough to hunt for Kelso.

While the narrow trail he had followed to this overlook was the quickest he knew, Slocum realized Kelso had explored every inch of the land and knew the terrain better than about anyone else. If the man had been in cahoots with the rustlers, he had followed every ridgeline and knew every hollow in these hills where strays might gather. Riding slowly, Slocum hunted for sign that Kelso had passed by recently.

He didn't find it. But he did see that he had been wrong about the spot where Kelso intended to watch the hanging. Some distance behind the cabin, in a stand of junipers mixed with taller cottonwoods, Slocum saw a flash of light reflected off metal. Using his field glasses, he waited until Kelso showed himself so he could be sure he wasn't seeing one of the posse lying in wait for Murphy.

Slocum studied the cabin and wondered if Murphy had already returned. There was no sign of anyone there, which heartened him. Putting away his binoculars, Slocum rode down the steep side of the hill and circled to get behind the grove where Kelso waited. It took longer than he thought, but Slocum didn't feel the pressure of time yet. Zamora and the posse hadn't shown up, nor had Seamus Murphy. Only when those two forces met would there be fireworks.

Dropping to the ground, Slocum let his horse wander away. He drew his six-shooter and advanced as silently as any Apache brave, slipping into the cool shadow of the trees. Every step had to be tested to be sure he wasn't breaking a twig or crunching down on dried leaves, which would warn Kelso. He need not have worried about alerting his former top hand. Kelso perched on the lowest limb of a cottonwood, intent on the cabin and nothing else. All Slocum had to do was aim and fire. He couldn't miss.

As quiet as a shadow slipping over a shadow, Slocum came up under where Kelso let his legs dangle down off the limb. His gun back in its holster, Slocum reached up and grabbed Kelso's boots and pulled as hard as he could. The man let out a loud cry of surprise, and grunted when he hit the ground hard. Lying facedown, Kelso had had the wind knocked out of him.

"You can roll over whenever you've got a mind to,"

Slocum said. "I've got you covered." He plucked Kelso's six-gun from its holster and tucked it into his belt.

"C-can't breathe."

"You won't be breathing much longer either if they lynch Murphy for something you've done."

"Ain't done nuthin'."

"You framed him for Wimmer's death."

"You cain't prove that."

"You set fire to the courthouse and tried to frame him for that, too."

"What's all this to you, Slocum? You got your big fancy ranch and a thousand head of cattle. What's it all to you if Murphy is lynched?"

"You really think getting rid of Murphy will improve your chances with Suzanne Underwood? She doesn't want a thing to do with you."

"So that's it," Kelso said, gasping hard. He sat up and glared at Slocum. "You figger you'll let the marshal hang Murphy, then pin all that on me so you'll get her. It won't work, Slocum. Suzanne loves me. She's just a mite confused, and you and Murphy are doin' it to her."

Slocum laughed harshly. Of all the people he had come across, Suzanne Underwood was hardly the one he would call confused. She knew what she wanted and would do anything to get it—even sleep with another man if it saved her beau. Slocum was slow to realize that Suzanne had been with him because she sought his help protecting Seamus Murphy, not because she found him desirable. That hurt bad, but Slocum appreciated her reasons. She had no friends and little else to offer to get a defender for Seamus Murphy.

Women had done far worse. And Slocum was looking at a man who'd certainly committed worse crimes to get what he wanted.

"Any reason I shouldn't plug you? You're not going to see Murphy hanged, one way or the other. If I can't stop the lynch mob, then I'll rob you of the pleasure of knowing your scheme worked."

"Go to hell, Slocum."

"Not before you." Slocum aimed his pistol and then looked up. Marshal Zamora and his men were riding up to Murphy's cabin.

"He's in there. I know he's in there, and the marshal'll get him. I'll die knowin' that I succeeded, not failed!"

Slocum stepped up and swung his pistol, laying the barrel alongside Kelso's head. The man went out like a light. Slocum hurried to the man's horse and got his lariat. It took several minutes to tie him up and lash him to the tree so he faced away from the cabin.

Then Slocum ran to the cabin, worried that Kelso might have told the truth for once. Seamus Murphy might be in the cabin and at risk of getting his neck stretched, unless Slocum could convince the mob he had the real culprit trussed up and waiting for them.

19

By the time Slocum reached Seamus Murphy's cabin, the posse had completely ringed it. Most had rifles or shotguns pointed at the walls, but Marshal Zamora and two others had six-shooters aimed at the only door into the cabin.

"Come on out or we start shooting," Zamora called.

"He's not in there," Slocum shouted. This got the marshal's attention, but the rest of the posse refused to budge. They kept their weapons trained on the cabin. He even heard one man grumbling about how much effort it would take to burn Murphy out. Another piped up that it would be worth doing since Murphy had tried to burn Heavenly to the ground.

"You butt out, Slocum. This is a matter for the law to handle."

"He's not there."

Zamora looked hesitant; then his jaw firmed and his lips thinned to a line. He spat a gob of chaw, held up his left hand to keep the posse where it was, then walked up and kicked in the door. The flimsy door slammed back and came off its hinges, falling down with a loud crash. Zamora jumped and almost opened fire. Then he came out of a crouch and went into the cabin.

Slocum followed. The room was empty.

"He didn't come back here," Slocum said. "He probably knew what would happen and didn't cotton much to a neck-tie party with him as the only guest."

"We'll find him. Truth is, he doesn't have anywhere else to run. If I have to, I can send out a dozen scouts and track him down."

"I caught the man responsible for everything," Slocum said. "Colorado Pete Kelso. He's the one who killed Jackson Wimmer and set fire to the courthouse to frame Murphy."

"Why'd he go and do a thing like that? He's a mean drunk—that I know from the times I tossed him in the clink—but what'd he gain by doing any of that?"

Slocum began his explanation, but the marshal was as stolid as the Rockies themselves and refused to believe a word of it.

Slocum walked slowly back to the tree where he had tied up Kelso. The man had struggled and had almost gotten free. Slocum took a few seconds to cinch down the rope again until Kelso complained.

"You're gonna cut off my damn hands that rope's so tight."

"You won't be needing your hands or much else when the law catches up with you," Slocum said. "All they'll need is a neck to put their noose around."

Kelso laughed harshly and said, "They're off huntin' fer Murphy, aren't they? I heard their horses ridin' off. A lot of them. You didn't turn me over 'cuz you knew you couldn't prove a thing."

"I don't much care about you starting a stampede and try-ing to kill me," Slocum said, looking down at the bound man. "Trying to frame Murphy for it with his kerchief is an-other matter."

"Nothin's illegal, even if I did it."

"You must have spent a powerful lot of time rooting around in Murphy's cabin."

"He's always out ridin' herd. That's the way it is when

you're a lone rancher. He couldn't even afford to hire a hand or two to help with the chores."

"So you rummaged through his belongings and took his bandanna and gun and hat."

"That hat." Kelso chuckled. "I thought that was a nice touch. Start the fire, leave it, then he'd get blamed. I didn't know he was inside the courthouse. That made it all the sweeter."

"How'd you know he was there?"

"After I set the fire, I watched. I considered takin' another shot or two at you, but you headed off to the creek. If you hadn't got the water pumpin', they'd have gone to see why. I needed enough time to get out of town."

"So you saw Murphy inside the courthouse?"

"Of course I did."

"Why'd you try to frame him for Wimmer's death? Because you didn't want to take the blame?"

"I had Murphy's six-shooter. Seemed the thing to do." Kelso laughed at the frame. "All I had to do was fire it."

"Into the ceiling?"

"Didn't want to shoot out through a window. I blasted a splinter out of the ceiling with Murphy's gun, then took the one beside Wimmer and hid it."

"You didn't use your own gun to kill Wimmer?"

"I didn't kill Wimmer. He was already dead. I heard the shot and went in. He was sprawled in the chair with a gun beside him. I saw my chance and took it."

"If you didn't kill him—" Slocum was cut off when Marshal Zamora pushed him aside.

"I heard enough. You got a big mouth, Kelso. I don't know if we can hang you for that, but you said enough to send you to jail for burning down the courthouse."

Kelso looked up. His mouth dropped open.

"I heard the horses. They left. You went with them."

"You thought he did," Slocum said. "I convinced him that Murphy wasn't the owlhoot he thought."

"But I wanted to make sure what Slocum told me wasn't just chin music. I've known a passel of men who could spin yarns that sounded good but were purebred lies. Not this time. You confessed of your own free will."

Kelso fought, but between the marshal and Slocum, they got him hog-tied and belly-down over his saddle.

"Reckon I ought to thank you, Slocum," Zamora said. "I got me a real criminal in Colorado Pete."

"No need to thank me, but you owe Seamus Murphy an apology."

"Well, it's likely to be a spell 'fore we see him again. If the man had a lick of sense, he's already in Wyoming and still ridin' hard."

"You said it, Marshal. If he had a lick of sense. He's got more to keep him here than the threat of dangling from a rope."

Marshal Zamora looked quizzically at Slocum, then led Kelso's horse with its human cargo back toward the cabin where his own horse was tethered. As Slocum watched them go, he chewed at his lower lip and thought hard. Kelso probably thought Wimmer had left *him* the Bar-S. With the owner dead, Kelso would be rich and powerful. And Kelso also thought that framing Murphy would be a way to get Suzanne Underwood.

Slocum walked back to find his horse, but he puzzled over Kelso's denial about having shot Wimmer. Kelso had discharged Murphy's six-shooter into the ceiling so it would look like the murder weapon, but why would he lie about killing Wimmer himself? He had boasted about every other crime he had committed. Murdering his boss would be a clever scheme in his twisted mind.

Slocum mounted and headed back down the road until he found the shortcut that led over the mountain onto Bar-S land. He had a herd to deliver to Montrose.

"We're almost there, Mr. Slocum. Another few miles and we're on the flats leading to the town," Ryan said.

"It's been an easy drive," Slocum said. "No rustlers or storms. Only the one problem."

"Cain't ever tell 'bout Colorado rivers. The Gunnison ran faster under the surface than I'd've thought for this late in the year. Still, we only lost a couple dozen head."

"Not bad for a herd of this size," Slocum said.

"You're soundin' mighty sad, if you don't mind my sayin' so. Somethin' eatin' at you, Mr. Slocum?"

"I've been thinking about the Bar-S all the way here and what I want to do," Slocum said.

"You fixin' to sell it?"

Slocum looked past Ryan to the other cowboys who had been loyal to him. They'd worked for Jackson Wimmer because he paid them. These men worked for John Slocum because they respected him. One or two, like Ryan and Jenks, he might even come to call friends—if he stayed on to run the ranch.

Being on the trail had reminded him what he liked so much. Under the bright Colorado sky he felt free. Sitting and filling out papers, worrying about bills, even with plenty of money to pay them, always sending men to do this chore or that . . . Slocum felt as if he had strung head-high barbed wire around himself at the Bar-S. The more he worked, the more he knew he belonged on the open range.

"I'm seriously considering it," Slocum said. He had no reason to lie to Ryan. "Keep it under your hat until after the herd's sold, will you?"

"Yes, sir, I will."

"I promise I won't sell to just anyone. He'll be a top-notch rancher."

"Wish I could step up and say that sounded like me, but it don't," Ryan said. "Truth is, being top hand is about all I'd want. Maybe foreman, but that's more 'n I want to think on right now."

"Right now, with the promise of a few silver dollars in your pocket, that's good enough."

"Yes, *sir.*"

Slocum laughed. He understood Ryan completely because that was the way *he* felt. It wasn't that he'd necessarily get roaring drunk, or even find himself a warm armful for the night, but he could feel that way. Ryan had his own moral code and could pass on such diversions. Slocum was free to choose whether to indulge or not. If he had a wife back on the Bar-S, he wouldn't be free to even think on such diversions after a long drive eating dust and listening to the mournful complaints of too many sides of beef on the hoof.

"Keep the herd here while I see to selling them," Slocum said.

He wanted to gallop into Montrose, but satisfied himself with a more stately walk. He looked around and saw a booming town serviced by a railroad. The people were pleasant and nodded to him as he rode, but there wasn't the friendliness that he felt in Heavenly the first time he had ridden in there. Slocum went to the stockyards near the railroad depot and looked for likely buyers.

He had expected two or three. He counted five.

On impulse, he went to the buyer with the smallest office, which was staffed by only two men. One, obviously the bookkeeper, looked as if he had not eaten in weeks. The other man looked up, gave Slocum a small grin, and came around a desk with his hand thrust out.

"Howdy. My name's Larkin. You lookin' to sell some cows?"

"I am, Mr. Larkin."

"I've got to warn you right off, I'm not the biggest shipper and I can't pay the most, but I am certainly the friendliest cuss in all of Montrose."

The bookkeeper grunted and turned back to his books.

Larkin said, "I usually say that I'm the handsomest, but my partner over there didn't like that."

"Reckon he wanted to claim that for himself," Slocum said.

The bookkeeper looked up, startled, then grinned. Larkin clapped Slocum on the back and ushered him to a seat at the desk.

"Now let's see what kind of a deal we can make to ship your beeves off to Denver."

The bargaining went on for the better part of the afternoon, but Slocum soon had twenty-five dollars a head for his cattle. After culling for breeding stock and taking into account those he had lost on the trail, Slocum pocketed $20,000. This wasn't the best price he could have gotten if he had gone to a larger buyer, but Slocum felt an obligation to do what he could to help those who were struggling to make good.

Somehow, although they looked nothing alike and their dispositions were like night and day, Larkin reminded Slocum of Seamus Murphy. Both men were tenacious and knew what they wanted out of life. He appreciated that.

He appreciated it even more when he realized he had come to a decision. He knew what he wanted out of life, too.

20

A lot had happened in the weeks Slocum had been on the trail, driving the cattle to market. Heavenly had a more cheerful aspect about it. Slocum rode directly to the marshal's office and went inside. Zamora sat behind his desk, reading a week-old copy of the *Rocky Mountain News*. He looked up when Slocum came in, and motioned toward the chair on the other side of the desk.

"Wondered when you'd get back," Zamora said.

"My curiosity got the better of me," Slocum said. He glanced toward the three cells at the rear of the jail. All were empty.

"Kelso got himself convicted of arson and a half dozen other crimes, including stealing from Seamus Murphy, and got sent to the prison over in Pueblo. Everyone was glad to see him go, though some were pissed that they didn't get a necktie party."

"They're not still thinking about Seamus Murphy for that honor, are they?"

"Nope." The marshal leaned back and laced his fingers behind his head. He looked as content as a cat with a bowl of fresh cream. "Things are real peaceful now in Heavenly. You might say the town's finally living up to its name."

"The rustlers are all driven off," Slocum said. "Other than the cattle saved over for the next year's herd, there's not a whole lot to draw the outlaws."

"Always some folks lookin' for a quick steak and easy meal, but they're nothing like a hardened rustler," the lawman agreed. "You looking for anyone in particular? The newly-weds?"

"Reckon so," Slocum said. "I wondered how long it would take for them to get hitched."

"Not more 'n a day or two after you hit the trail. I have to say, that made folks a whole lot friendlier toward them. Now maybe if somebody's got an ache or pain, they'll take it to Doc Gainsborough instead of the vet. He was gettin' mighty tired of seein' more human patients than four-legged ones."

Slocum put on his best poker face. This was not what he had expected to hear.

"Where might the happy couple be right now?"

"Over at the doc's office."

"Marshal," Slocum said, "I wish you nothing but the best in keeping the peace."

Zamora chuckled, then rocked forward so he could plant his elbows on the desk and continue reading his newspaper. Slocum left and went directly to Ben Gainsborough's office.

"Mr. Slocum, heard you were back," Doc Gainsborough greeted. "Come on in, pull up a chair, and let's share a nip of . . . medicine." He looked at Nora from the corner of his eye to see how she responded. She made a sour face and waved him to go on. "That's why I married her. She understands that a man's got to sample a taste of whiskey now and then, call it medicine or just plain camaraderie."

"You *just* married her?" Slocum took the amber liquid and sloshed it around in the water glass. Gainsborough had poured a hefty drink. With a single swift gulp, Slocum downed it. The liquor burned down to his belly and sat warming his innards.

"Slocum, you've been here for a while but you don't know squat about the people. Nora and I, we, well—"

"Get to the point, Ben. He's not a child." Nora Gainsborough looked at the whiskey bottle as if damning it for her husband's reluctance. "We were not married but lived together in sin."

Slocum knew that already. He had another question that burned the tip of his tongue as he asked.

"For how long?" Slocum saw Nora and Ben exchange looks.

"Close to fifteen years, give or take," she said. "This is why the townspeople avoided Ben when they had medical problems."

"That's why they went to the vet," Slocum said, remembering what the marshal had told him.

Gainsborough chuckled and sipped at his whiskey. "He got more business than I did sometimes. I thought about taking up his line of work. No foaling season could be as hard as working on a patient who thought I was Satan's tool."

"His bedmate," Nora corrected.

"Why'd you just get married after all these years?" Even as the words left his mouth, Slocum knew the answer. "Jackson Wimmer died," he said in answer to his own question.

"The son of a bitch refused to divorce me. He was all about controlling everyone around him. He made money from the Bar-S, as you probably know going over his books, but more than this, he never gave up power. Ever." Tears welled in Nora's eyes. She put her hand on her new husband's shoulder.

"You could have moved somewhere else where they didn't know you," Slocum pointed out.

"No, I couldn't."

"Her daughter wanted to stay near her pa, though he treated her worse than anyone else after Nora left him."

Slocum reached for the whiskey and poured another jolt as strong as the first. Only after he had swallowed a considerable portion of it did he trust himself to ask, "Suzanne?"

"Our daughter, mine and Jackson's. We left him when she was five."

Slocum remembered the picture on the office wall and how Kelso had taken it for no reason he could tell. Now he could. Kelso was obsessed with Suzanne Underwood, and had either found out or recognized her as a small child with Wimmer. He had taken the picture as a trophy after killing Wimmer, probably as a show of devotion to Suzanne.

"She doesn't have anything good to say about him. But why does she go by the name Underwood?"

"That's my maiden name. I suppose it was the only way she could think to make it seem, at least to her, that she had disowned us all."

"I saw that plainly. She acted like she was walking on hot coals the times she was in the ranch house," Slocum said.

Gainsborough's eyebrows arched. "She went there? She vowed she would never go there as long as he was alive."

Slocum went cold inside as pieces of the puzzle fell into place for him.

"She killed her pa, didn't she? She shot Wimmer."

"No!" Both Nora and Ben shouted at the same time.

"Then Kelso must have, only he didn't brag on it. A man like that would."

Again, Nora and Ben exchanged looks. Gainsborough supplied the key that Slocum lacked.

"You know he was all eaten up inside with cancer. I showed you what remained of his stomach over at the undertaker's," Gainsborough said. He studied Slocum a moment, then went on. "It's hard to prove, but I think Wimmer killed himself. He couldn't stand the pain anymore, and it wouldn't have been long before he began wasting away to nothing."

"He was already skin and bones," Slocum said, remembering how light Wimmer had been when he picked him up after the rancher had been shot. He should have realized Wimmer was sick then, but the old codger's sharp tongue had kept the conversation away from such observations at the time.

"A man like him, always in control, he could never tolerate

being beholden to someone else to feed or fetch for him because he was unable to do it himself." Nora moved behind Ben and put both hands on his stooped shoulders, as much to comfort herself as him, Slocum thought.

"So Kelso only took advantage of the situation?"

"The best we can figure, he heard the shot, found Wimmer dead, then left Seamus's gun to implicate him," Gainsborough said. "You answered why Kelso had the gun."

"A trophy. He fired the gun into the ceiling so it would have a round spent, then took Wimmer's so nobody would ask why there were two guns that had just been fired. That was a mistake. If he had left it, it might have looked like he and Murphy struggled and fought it out."

"That might get Murphy off with a self-defense plea. This way it looked as if Wimmer was murdered."

"The old son of a bitch checked out by his own hand, and Kelso took advantage." Slocum finished his whiskey. "You know about your daughter and Murphy?"

"They've made no secret of how they feel about each other," Nora said. A tiny smile crept across her lips. "Like mother, like daughter, I reckon. At first I thought she took up with Seamus just to thumb her nose at everyone in town, including me."

"You and her don't get on very well?"

"She never forgave me for a lot of things. She was young when I left Jackson, but she was a complete pariah in town as a result of me taking up with Ben. She grew up being snubbed and blamed Ben here for it because I loved him so. That might be why she and Seamus are so good together. She's with another outcast."

"They just might be like two peas in a pod," Slocum said.

"He's a hothead, and she might be a calming influence on him. Opposites, not kindred spirits."

There was a touch of wistfulness in her tone that made Slocum sit up. His mind raced as choices surfaced and sank.

"You reckon they're out at his ranch?"

Nora shrugged. Gainsborough said, "Last I heard, he had filed for a marriage license. With the fire and all, I don't know if the clerk's had time to do much about it."

"What Ben means, Seamus is still as much a pariah as ever. There's been plenty of time for them to get their records in order and they haven't done it. Suzanne didn't even come into town when Ben and me got hitched."

"Nobody showed up, 'cept the judge," Gainsborough said. "And Gutherie. He was a witness. Never expected that from him, but who's gonna cross the man who owns both the general store and saloon?"

"I might be able to speed up things." Slocum got to his feet. "Don't go off for a while. I'll be back."

Slocum went to the courthouse and saw how it had been repaired in his absence. It took the better part of an hour for him to find everything he needed, going from one clerk to another. Then he went to the bank before returning to Gainsborough's office. Slocum didn't take the offered chair or glass of whiskey this time.

He handed Nora Gainsborough a sealed envelope and said, "Don't open this until the right time."

"Right time for what?" She looked confused as she ran her fingers over the stuffed envelope.

"You'll know," Slocum said. He shook hands with Ben Gainsborough and nodded to Nora, then left.

He mounted and knew he had one more stop to make. Slocum found the turnoff from the main road and headed into the hills, using the shortcut that would take him to Seamus Murphy's cabin. He reached the lonely cabin an hour before sundown to find Murphy standing in the doorway with his six-shooter in his hand. Slocum had been spotted riding up.

"You get on outta here, Slocum. You're not welcome."

"Don't hurt yourself with that hogleg," Slocum said, stepping down from his horse. "I want a word with you."

"They sent you. I know they sent you to throw me off my land. You're not gonna do it."

"We won't let you," Suzanne said. "We're in this together, and we won't let you throw us off."

"I talked it over with the clerk. If you still want that marriage license, just ask."

"Don't meddle, Slocum. I don't need you meddling. Next thing I know, you'll be buyin' the Circle M note from the bank and giving it to me as a wedding present."

"We wouldn't accept it!"

"The thought never crossed my mind," Slocum said. "Your problems with the Circle M are yours and none of my business."

"Then get out. I got work to do if I'm gonna keep this place."

"You'd do anything to make a success of it?"

"Yes," both Suzanne and Seamus said as one. Slocum forced himself to keep from smiling as he recollected how Nora and Ben Gainsborough had answered simultaneously, too. They were as much of one mind as these two were.

"I never thought I'd ever be a rancher and certainly not own a spread the size of the Bar-S." Slocum looked hard at Suzanne and said, "Your pa named the spread after you, didn't he? Bar-S? Bar-Suzanne?"

"It was his way of keeping his thumb pressed down on me."

"Might be," Slocum allowed. "Might be he was proud of you being his daughter. But that's not what I wanted to say."

Slocum waited to build a little tension. He got it. Suzanne pressed closer to her man, and Murphy fingered his six-shooter. Both looked anxiously at Slocum.

"I'm not cut out to run a ranch the size of the Bar-S. Truth is, the longer I stay there, the more I want to just ride away."

"So why don't you do it?" Suzanne asked.

"I intend to, but getting the ranch as a legacy that wasn't mine wears down on me. I'm letting you have first chance at buying the Bar-S from me."

Murphy laughed harshly.

"There's no way I could buy a ranch that big and successful. I can't even meet the mortgage on the Circle M."

"I said I don't care what happens here. You can buy the Bar-S for five thousand dollars."

"You might as well have asked for a million dollars. That's as far out of my reach as five thousand."

"Borrow the money," Slocum said.

"Nobody in town's gonna loan me a plugged nickel, much less that much. If they would, I'd have paid off the note on my own place."

"Buy the Bar-S and I reckon you'll have the banker begging you to take out a bigger loan or even giving you a break on the one you've got. The more money you have, the more bankers want to give you money," Slocum said.

"Who?" asked Murphy. "Who has that much?"

Slocum looked at Suzanne. She recoiled and shook her head when she read the answer in his face. Murphy still didn't know.

"Your ma might have that much. Ask her."

"I won't be in her debt."

"Would that be so bad? You could pay her back in one good season and own the Bar-S free and clear. The Circle M butts up against Bar-S land. The two ranches together would be even more profitable. I've seen some of your pasture. Looks good."

"Your high pastures are better," Murphy said.

"They could be yours. You up to a challenge like that?"

"I'd need ranch hands," Murphy said.

"It'd be real hard keeping the ones that worked the Bar-S this season," Slocum said, "because I gave each of the ten a five-hundred-dollar bonus. They'd be looking for that much again, if the ranch was successful."

"If you could give them that big a bonus, why are you selling?" Suzanne stood beside Seamus now, and forced his hand with the six-gun down.

"I'll have more money in my pocket than I've ever had."

"The five thousand we'd pay you," Suzanne said. Slocum saw her turning over the possibilities in her mind.

"All the debts are paid from profit from this year's herd. You'd be starting even, except for the loan."

"From my ma."

"From your ma," Slocum agreed.

Suzanne's expression changed and she said, "You must have really itchy feet to give up the Bar-S like this."

"I do," Slocum said.

"Shake on it, Seamus," Suzanne said. "We're buying ourselves a ranch."

"If your mother has the money," Seamus Murphy said skeptically.

"She does," Slocum said.

Durango was only another day's ride ahead of him. Occasionally, Slocum fought the urge to turn around and go back toward Heavenly, but he'd resisted the first couple days on the trail, and now the longing to be on the Bar-S again was slowly fading.

He had done well for himself. Suzanne and Seamus had gone to Nora Gainsborough and smoothed over differences that were caused by pride and the need to find someone to strike out against. What Slocum had not counted on was Seamus Murphy's insistence on putting a price on the Bar-S twice what Slocum had asked. The five-thousand-dollar balance would be paid to Slocum in ten payments, deposited in the Heavenly bank over the next decade. If he ever needed money, he reckoned he could return to Heavenly once a year and then ride off again with a new bankroll.

Or he could let the money pile up. He had spoken with the banker. When Seamus and Suzanne had children, they just might find accounts in their name. Slocum knew Nora would see that the banker remained honest.

He patted the wad of greenbacks in his pocket and glanced back at his saddlebags where gold coins rested, all in payment for a ranch he had never wanted. He might miss Ryan, who had accepted the job as foreman from Seamus Murphy, and riding land that was his, and the sight of a thousand head of fine cattle being driven to the railhead in his name, but he doubted it. Along with moments like that came fighting rustlers, stringing endless miles of barbed wire, worrying about things he no longer had to even consider.

Slocum tapped his mare's flanks and got the horse moving a little faster. He had no idea what he would find in Durango, but it had nothing to do with the hundreds of problems of running a ranch.

Once more he was free, and it felt good, damned good.

Watch for

SLOCUM AND EL LOCO

360th novel in the exciting SLOCUM series
from Jove

Coming in February!

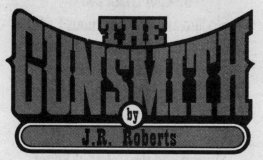